Brief Encounters

Also by Edna Taylor and published by Ginninderra Press
Skeleton in the Cupboard

Edna Taylor

Brief Encounters

This second book is dedicated to all those people
who read the first one and asked for more.

It is also a thank you to my friends at the Creative Writing
Group for their encouragement and help in my decision to
continue this strangely compulsive journey of writing, and for
the love of the written word, which has no boundaries.

Brief Encounters
ISBN 978 1 76041 024 7
Copyright © text Edna Taylor 2015
Cover photo © Fotoschlick – Fotolia

First published 2015 by
GINNINDERRA PRESS
PO Box 3461 Port Adelaide SA 5015
www.ginninderrapress.com.au

Contents

A Feast

'If music be the food of love, play on.' The old saying suddenly popped unbidden into Sadie Perkin's head. She didn't know where she had heard it before but it seemed to fit the moment.

She was hiding behind the curtain in front of the side door leading into the theatre. She wasn't supposed to be there. Sadie was employed by a firm of cleaners who tidied up the theatre after the show had finished and the audience had left.

Today the orchestra was giving a matinee concert. They were playing Rachmaninoff's second piano concerto with a well known pianist. Sadie had found a discarded programme left on a seat from the previous night's performance. She could never have afforded to pay for a seat in the theatre nowadays, but she loved to listen to the old classics and had CDs of all her favourites which she treasured.

Sadie had recently discovered that this particular door was not locked, and was only used as an emergency exit. So she had summoned her courage and slipped in there this afternoon when all the audience had been settled in their seats and there was no one left outside.

Sadie had stood up for a while. It was only a small space, about a metre wide, but enough room for her. She had been ready to make a run for it in case anyone decided to check the door, but so far so good. She could hear everyone settling down and gradually quieten as the lights dimmed, and then the orchestra started with the opening bars. She longed to have a look through the curtain but didn't dare, as one of the ushers could be standing close by, so it wasn't worth the risk. She could hear just fine, though, so she settled herself on the carpeted floor and gave herself up to the glorious music. Sadie felt transported with joy, she felt a rapturous bliss which was so overwhelming and beautiful she could hardly bear it.

For nearly a couple of hours, Sadie forgot the seemingly

insurmountable problems with her life, and when the last notes finally died away and the applause started, she couldn't move for a moment. She was still so completely transfixed, but then she had to struggle to get to her feet, realising that she had to hurry out of there before everyone started leaving.

She cautiously opened the door and peeked out. There was no one in sight, so she quickly left, making her way to the staff room where the other girls were waiting to go to work in the theatre.

'You look happy, Sadie,' remarked someone. 'What have you been up to then?'

She wanted to say, 'Having a feast of lovely music,' but she knew they wouldn't understand, and anyway Sadie wasn't about to share her hiding place with anyone.

'Nothing much,' she said. 'I just had a lovely late lunch with an old friend.'

The Gift

The guests were gone. The party was over, and there was a big mess to clean up. All the presents were stacked on a side table.

Sally settled back onto the couch with a sigh. 'That was a great party, wasn't it?' She sounded tired but happy.

'It was a good idea of yours to have a house-warming,' her partner Bob called back from the kitchen where he was starting to clean up. 'Everyone has been so kind. I never thought we would have got so much stuff.'

'Leave that for now,' she said. 'Come and have a drink and we'll clean it up later. There's still a present to open.' Sally reached over to the table and picked up an unopened parcel sitting among all the opened gifts.

Bob poured the last of a bottle of red into a glass and sat down. 'Who's that from then?' he asked.

Sally was looking a bit dumbfounded at the parcel. It was wrapped in newspaper, and tied with string. 'I don't know,' she said. 'There's no tag or anything. I have no idea where this could have come from.' She shook it gently. 'Doesn't rattle.'

'Oh yes, I remember now, somebody found it on the doorstep and brought it in with them,' remarked Bob, 'I forget who it was.'

Indeed, there had been a few people there who Bob didn't recognise. They were folks from the Helping Hand centre where Sally volunteered once a week. This was a drop-in centre where people could have a cuppa and meet with other folks for a chat, a game of cards and so on. There were quite a few elderly people without family who were regulars and Sally loved to chat with them. Sometimes she would invite people home for a meal, as had happened in this case. She and Bob had recently moved into the big old house which the salesman had called a renovator's dream, but it had been a bargain. Bob had started on the renovations and it was beginning to look rather better than it had when they had moved in, so they had decided it was time for a house-warming party.

Sally started unwrapping the parcel. It was quite big, about fifty centimetres square. There was more newspaper inside and Sally took it off, finally revealing a painting in a beautiful antique wooden carved frame.

They were both speechless for a moment. Sally peered at the name, just discernible, written into the bottom right-hand corner. 'Edward Greenaway, 1960,' she read.

'My goodness.' Bob looked at it closely. 'Who on earth?'

Sally was holding it reverently. 'It's beautiful.' She brushed it gently with her fingers. 'It's oils, and it's old, and considering it was painted in 1960 the colours are still bright and lovely.'

Indeed, it was a well executed painting of a landscape, containing a derelict looking pioneer hut with a background which looked like the Flinders Ranges.

'I wonder who left this for us,' wondered Sally. 'We don't know who to thank.'

'Well,' said Bob, 'I expect we'll find out sooner or later. Somebody will own up. In the meantime, we could hang it on that spare hook in the hall.'

So that's where they put it, and it was just the right spot, the light catching it every time the front door was opened.

Next door to Sally and Bob there lived an elderly gentleman. Sally had met him the day before when she had been backing out the car to go to the shops to get things for their house-warming. He had been struggling along the path to the mailbox. The postie had just been. The old chap seemed rather frail and was leaning heavily on his walking stick. He fumbled with the door on the mailbox and a letter fell out onto the footpath.

Sally had noticed, so she had stopped the car, jumped out and quickly ran across to the gate. 'Hold on,' she said. 'I'll get that for you.'

She bent and picked up the letter and handed it to him. 'I don't think we've met,' she added. 'I'm Sally. Wwe've just moved in next door. Me and my partner Bob. I'm so pleased to meet you.'

The old gentleman seemed a little overawed, and blinked at the sturdy young woman with short blonde hair, friendly blue eyes and a big smile. He peered at Sally behind thick spectacles. 'Thank you,' he said.

'I'm afraid I don't know your name,' she said.

He looked warily at her. 'Just call me Ted,' he said softly and turned to make his way back along the path.

A sudden impulse made Sally call after him. 'We're having a house-warming tonight. You'd be very welcome.'

But he ignored her. Or perhaps, she thought, his hearing wasn't so good. This was the first time she had seen her reclusive neighbour. She wondered whether he would like to go and meet some folks at the Helping Hand. But now was obviously not a good time. She would maybe talk to him about that later.

Ted had a smile on his face. It was the first time anyone had spoken to him for a long time, apart from the Meals on Wheels people, who barely passed the time of day. They just left the meal and went. They were always in such a hurry.

He went into the back of the house and looked at all the old paintings stacked against the wall in a spare room. He hadn't painted anything for a very long time. His failing sight and the arthritis had put paid to that. Now and again the man from the gallery came around and bought one, and it was the sales of these pictures that had helped keep him going these past few years. The numbers were dwindling now; most of the big ones were gone. He wondered whether that pleasant young lady would like a painting for her house-warming party. Sally, wasn't it? Such a nice person, he thought. So kind. He had indeed heard her invitation, but Ted rarely left the house. He kept himself to himself. He knew he was regarded by the locals as an eccentric old bloke. He didn't mind. He preferred it that way.

Ted looked around at the paintings, finally selected one and carefully dusted it off with a rag. It took him quite a while to wrap it up and his arthritic hands didn't much like having to tie a knot in the string, but he managed. He hoped Sally would like it.

When the meals on wheels people came that lunchtime, he asked one of them if they would kindly leave it next door. Which they did, but no one was home, so they had left it on the doorstep.

One morning, Sally's friend Jane dropped by for a quick coffee. She had previously noticed the painting on the wall and had remarked how nice she thought it was. Now she had an air of excitement about her. 'Guess what!' she exclaimed.

Sally smiled. 'Just tell me, what is it?'

Jane couldn't contain herself. 'It's your painting. The one you didn't know who had sent it. Did you ever find out who it was?'

'No,' Sally shook her head. 'Still haven't a clue. Why, do you know something I don't?'

'Yes,' exclaimed Jane. 'I've seen one by the same artist, Edward Greenaway. In that little gallery in Comber Street just north of the city. The bus stop is right outside and I popped in there to pass the time until the bus was due. It was just by luck I happened to notice it. Guess how much it's on sale for. It's an oil, a little bit bigger than the one you've got.' Jane stopped to take a breath.

Sally was intrigued. 'Go on then, how much?'

'A thousand dollars.'

'What?' Sally gasped. 'Are you sure it's by the same artist?'

'Quite sure. In fact, it's a similar sort of painting, Australiana, outback sort of thing. Quite beautiful. If I could afford to, I'd buy it.'

Sally couldn't say anything for a minute. She took a long sip of her coffee, deep in thought. 'But who on earth do we know who could afford to give us such a valuable painting?'

'It's a bit of a mystery, isn't it?' Jane drank the last of her coffee. 'Anyway, I just thought you'd like to know. I've got to run now. I'll catch up with you again later.' Then she was gone.

Typical Jane, thought Sally, always enjoys dropping bombshells and then going. But now she was intrigued. She knew the gallery Jane had referred to and resolved to pay them a visit.

Next day was Saturday and she had some free time. She drove to the city and found a car park close to the gallery. She peered through the window for a minute and looked at the paintings displayed there. They were all quite expensive, far beyond her reach, and Sally hoped they didn't try to sell her anything. But she needn't have worried. No one approached her as she looked around. There was a lady sitting at a desk at the back who was talking on a phone and took little or no notice of Sally as she wandered about. She soon found the painting Jane was talking about, and indeed there was another one as well for the same price.

Sally made a decision. She waited until the woman had apparently finished her call and approached the desk. 'Excuse me,' she started. 'I'm just wondering about those paintings by Edward Greenaway.'

The woman jumped up and gave a big smile. 'Oh yes, Greenaway. We have two of his lovely works here. Which one would you be interested in?'

'Um,' Sally didn't want to get the woman's hopes up. 'I don't actually want to purchase one. In fact, I already have one of his works at home.'

The woman's eyebrows shot up in surprise and a look of respect crept over her face as she realised that here was a connoisseur of fine art. 'Well now, what can I do for you, madam?'

It was a long time since Sally had been called madam. She stood up a little straighter and tried to look like someone who went around purchasing expensive paintings. 'I would like to find out a bit more about the artist,' she said. 'Do you sell many of his works?'

'Well, not so many these days, though we have sold quite a few in the past.' The woman's smile had dropped a little. 'We sell more of the modern abstract. All I know about Mr Greenaway is that he's a local resident. I've never met him personally. Mr Jenkins, our scout, is always on the lookout for paintings, and I believe he may have purchased some from Mr Greenaway.'

'I see.' Jane thought quickly. 'I wonder…' she started when the gallery door opened and a man entered carrying a large wrapped-up parcel.

'Oh, talk of the devil.' The gallery person turned towards the man. 'Hello, Bert. That's good timing. I' like to introduce…' she turned to Sally. 'I'm sorry, I don't know your name.'

'It's Sally, Sally Porter.' She put out her hand. 'Pleased to meet you.'

'Bert Jenkins,' said the man. He shook her hand, held on longer than was necessary and gave her a quick once over. He turned his attention to the gallery lady. 'Hi, Betty, just got another one for you. Deceased estate. There'll be more where that's come from, depending on what you think. Nice to meet you,' he smiled at Sally, his eyes resting on her a little too long. 'I'll just put this in the back and give it a bit of a clean-up,' he added.

'Excuse me.' Sally wasn't about to miss this opportunity, even if he made her feel uncomfortable. 'Have you met Edward Greenaway, the artist?'

'Why do you want to know?' He sounded wary.

'I have one of his paintings. It was a gift,' she added quickly, 'and I wanted to know about him. I like his work,' she added.

Bert Jenkins thought quickly. Ted Greenaway was one of his regulars. He had a good thing going which was no one else's business. 'Sorry love…er ,Sally,' he corrected himself, 'this particular artist wants to remain anonymous. I am not at liberty to give you his address. Sorry,' he said again, not looking the least bit sorry. Then he turned and quickly headed for the back of the shop.

'I'm sorry too, Sally.' Betty turned towards the desk on which the phone had started ringing. I'm afraid I can't help you. Will you excuse me?' She turned around, no longer interested in someone who obviously wasn't about to purchase anything.

Sally nodded and made her way to the door. She drove back home feeling a little despondent. Too late, she realised she should have asked Betty who was the last person she sold a Greenaway painting to. But there again, she thought, whoever had given the painting to them might have had it for years. She wondered why Bert Jenkins had acted a bit weird when she had mentioned Edward Greenaway.

That night Sally got on to the computer and googled Edward Greenaway, and wondered why she hadn't thought of that before, but there was nothing; he wasn't listed.

Strangely, as it happened, next Monday by chance, Sally met the postie at the mailbox when she was putting the garbage bin out.

'G'day,' he greeted her in his usual cheerful manner. 'Do you know if Mr Greenaway is away? He didn't collect his mail on Friday.' Indeed, there was a magazine or something stuck in the opening.

And just like that she realised. 'Ted?' she asked. 'Is that Mr Greenaway?'

'Yes, love.' The postie gave her a curious look as he regarded her surprised expression. 'That's him.'

Sally stood stock-still for a moment then quickly gathered herself. 'I don't know,' she said. 'I haven't seen him for a bit. She held out her hand. 'I'll take his mail and see if he's OK.'

'Thanks, love, that'd be kind of you. You never know with these old folks.' He was revving up his bike, eager to get going, and gave her a wave.

Sally opened the mailbox, extracted the catalogue and collected the mail, there wasn't much, then she made her way up the garden path to Ted's front door. She stopped, took a deep breath and knocked gently. It seemed to be very quiet inside. She put her ear to the door, but could hear nothing. So, determined now to find out what was going on, she made her way round the side of the house to the back door. She raised her hand to knock, and the door moved. It was open. Sally had a feeling of dread as she stepped into the kitchen and looked around. On the table were unopened Meals on Wheels food containers.

Then she called out again. 'Are you there, Ted? Are you OK?'

Then a small sound came from a room leading off the kitchen. 'In here.'

Heaving a sigh of relief, Sally gave a quick knock and opened the bedroom door. 'It's just me, Sally, from next door. Just checking if you're OK.' She went over to the bed. 'I can see you're not.' She put a hand on his forehead. 'My goodness, you're burning up. How long have you been like this?'

'Just a coupla days. I'll be right,' Ted whispered. He could scarcely speak. 'It's just the flu. Thank you for coming.'

He was overcome by a fit of coughing and that was enough for Sally. She was already on her mobile and calling an ambulance.

The ambos were great. They put him on a ventilator and congratulated Sally on acting so quickly. Another day and it might have been a different story, they said.

That night, she and Bob were discussing the whole amazing business.

'Just think,' she said, 'it was Ted all the time. Who would have thought? Anyway, he's in good hands now. I hope he's going to be all right. When he comes home, we'll have to think of a way to thank him for the painting.'

Next day, Sally went back into Ted's house. 'Don't worry, Ted,' she had said as they tucked him into the ambulance. 'I'll lock up and keep an eye on everything.'

Which of course she did. She also cleaned the house, chucked out rotten food stuffs, and thought to ring up Meals on Wheels, who told her they had put Friday's meal on the kitchen table as usual and had assumed Ted was in the bathroom as sometimes happened. He always left the back door open for them, they said, and now they were sorry they hadn't checked more thoroughly.

Sally also had a peek in the back room and discovered all the paintings stacked up around the walls. She thought about Bert Jenkins, who apparently bought Ted's paintings and sold them to the gallery. She also wondered how much he was paying Ted for his work. By the look of the poor conditions in which the old chap lived, he certainly wasn't making much out of it.

Ted stayed in hospital for ten days before being allowed home. Sally had been to see him a couple of times, and the nurse told her that she had been the only visitor.

'I'll keep an eye on him,' she had told the nurse, who was concerned for his welfare after he had been discharged. By now, Sally was feeling quite protective of the old gentleman.

After he came home from the hospital, she invited him round for a meal, resolved to bring up the subject of his paintings. At first, he demurred, saying it would be too much trouble, that he didn't go out much, that he was fine and that she was not to bother about him. But Sally persisted and in the end he came for dinner one evening.

'Now,' Sally started, when they were settled and they all had a plate of roast chicken in front of them. 'First of all, Ted, we want to thank you for the lovely painting. We didn't know who it was from. It had no note or anything.'

Ted had noticed the painting in the hall when Sally had welcomed him into their home, and was quietly pleased to see it hanging there. 'Oh, sorry,' was all he could manage to say. Indeed, it had never occurred to him to write a note; he had been happy to remain anonymous.

'Never mind, Ted, it's OK,' Bob smiled. 'At least we know now and we just wanted to say thank you.'

Sally nodded.

Ted wasn't much for small talk and had started on his chicken, which he realised was much better than the Meals on Wheels food.

'Ted?' Sally looked a little hesitant, at what she was about to say. 'I've seen some of your paintings in the Comber Street Gallery.'

Ted nodded. 'I guess that's where that feller Bert takes them.'

Sally persisted. 'Do you know how much they sell them for?'

Ted shook his head, 'No, never asked, never been there.'

'A thousand dollars,' she said.

'A thousand?' Ted jerked a little and dropped his knife onto the plate.

Sally laid her hand gently on his arm. 'Ted, do you mind if I ask you – not that it's any of my business – but how much does he pay you for your paintings? Are you getting a proper price?'

Ted was quiet for a long moment. 'A hundred and fifty,' he said at last. 'He told me that the frames were worth more than the pictures.'

Sally and Bob both looked so aghast that neither could speak.

Then Sally burst out with 'That's disgusting, that's unbelievable. Ted, you're getting ripped off.' She was so angry, indignant that anyone could take advantage of a dear old chap like Ted. 'Well, we'll see about that, won't we, Bob.' She glanced at her mate ,who looked just as angry, which was unusual in such a laid-back guy who never got upset about anything.

So Sally got to work. First another visit to the gallery to talk to Betty, who she thought probably wouldn't know what Bert was up to.

'Do you know that Bert only pays Ted a hundred and fifty dollars for his paintings?' Sally demanded to know.

'What?' Betty was immediately up in arms. 'Don't be ridiculous.'

'How much do you pay Bert?'

'That's none of your business.'

'It is my business when one of my friends is getting ripped off.'

Betty was looking decidedly uncomfortable. 'It's the same for everyone,' she said. 'The gallery gets thirty per cent commission on sales, which means the owner of the painting gets seventy per cent.'

Sally worked it out quickly. 'Then Bert gets seven hundred dollars each time you sell Mr Greenaway's thousand-dollar paintings?'

'Well, yes,' Betty hastened to distance herself from Bert Jenkins's shady dealings, 'but how was I to know what he pays for the paintings?'

Sally said nothing. She was so disgusted to think that the owner of a gallery, even a small one such as this, would have not have made more enquiries about the original artist whose work she was selling.

Betty was worried now. She wondered whether Bert was doing similar deals with other artists. 'I'll have a talk with him,' she said.

'You do that,' Sally answered, 'and here's my phone number.' She handed Betty a note. 'I'd appreciate it if you'd let me know what Bert has to say for himself.'

She phoned the gallery a couple of days later. There had been no word from Betty and she was soon to find out why. Bert, it seemed, had disappeared. His phone had been disconnected. Betty had been sufficiently worried to visit the address that Bert had given her, but he was no longer there. She tracked down the landlord of the rented units, who told her that Bert Jenkins had left without leaving a forwarding address.

'Which is just as well,' said Sally. 'Maybe he's decided to cut his losses and not take a chance that some nosy parker like me might start investigating his business dealings.'

Sally took Ted to the gallery to meet Betty, who made a great effort to be as nice as possible, assuring him that he would get his full percentage of any future sales. She even agreed to have a special showing of all the rest of Ted's work at present residing in his back room.

So it all turned out rather well. Ted was quite overawed with the amount of the generous cheque he eventually received from proceeds of the gallery sale. He had even agreed to visit the Helping Hand centre due to Sally's insistence that he needed to get out more.

'But there's no guarantee, mind,' he told Sally. 'I'm used to my own company, I don't need to mix with other folks.'

Sally had smiled to herself. As she later told Bob, 'There's this lovely little old lady who goes to the Helping Hand centre and has always wanted to learn to paint…'

The Black Cat

If you're superstitious, you may believe that black cats are unlucky. They say that if one crosses your path then beware, all sorts of bad things could happen to you. Some people believe they're lucky. I am not superstitious, therefore I didn't believe anything untoward would happen when I opened my front door and saw a black cat sitting outside the front gate. When I opened it to go through, the cat didn't budge. So I stepped over it, turned and closed the gate again.

I stopped for a moment and looked down to see large green eyes gazing at me with a strangely intense expression. I stepped back and froze for a moment, then common sense took over. It was, after all, just a cat which was probably lost. As I had to get to the bus stop and didn't have much time to spare that morning, I hurried away. I couldn't resist a look back, though, to see if it was still there. It was; it was watching me walk away.

It was a bit creepy and I thought about the black cat all the way to work, and then forgot it during the busyness of the day. Therefore it wasn't until I was coming home again that evening that I remembered the cat. I hoped it would be gone, but as soon as I turned the corner, a little flick of my pulse told me it was still there, exactly where I had last seen it, right outside the gate. It was lying down, curled up into a neat little ball. When it heard me coming, it got up, stretched and stood up, facing me as I approached. It looked just as though it had been waiting for me. As I reached it and stopped to open the gate, it sidled up and rubbed itself against my legs, purring loudly.

Well, what could I do? This cat had apparently decided this was where he or she wanted to be. I was torn. I had no desire for a cat. I had never wanted a cat. If I had an animal at all, it would have been a dog. I had lived alone for a long time with no one and nothing to worry about except myself. A cat would be a burden. There would be kitty litter trays, and scratch marks over the furniture. Extra food to buy. I didn't know anything about cat food. All the negatives of having a cat went through my head, but I also couldn't bear to see animals badly treated. I thought that if I left it outside tonight it might be gone in the morning, but on the other hand it might be cold and hungry, and I would probably worry about it. I looked down at it and those green eyes gazed back at me.

'OK,' I said. 'Come on then.'

I opened the gate and the cat went through. Its tail was up and it walked with an air of propriety, looking from side to side as though inspecting the garden. Already it seemed to have taken ownership. It stopped by the front door and, as soon as I opened it, disappeared inside. Bemused, I followed behind. Straight to the kitchen it went, walked around as if checking everything out. Then it went into the hall, through to the living room and back out, where it stopped in front of the stairs.

Quite amused now, I said, 'Well, feel free. You can go upstairs if you want to.'

It gave one look at me then sedately went up the stairs. I followed, and even opened the door so that it could look in the bedroom.

What are you doing? I said to myself. You are actually giving a cat a tour of your house. How stupid can you be. It all seemed very strange and indeed funny at the time.

Anyway, I left it there exploring the place and went back downstairs and into the kitchen, where I put the kettle on for coffee and started defrosting some chicken to cook for tea. When I went to look for the cat, I found it curled up on the rug in the living room. There was no doubt about it: this strange black cat had made itself at home.

I thought I should give it a name. But it was difficult to know whether it was male or female. It was big, black and shiny. Its coat seemed to be in good condition and it didn't seem to be underfed, but it was hard to tell under all that hair. I thought it looked more like a boy, so I called it Tom. My grandad had a black cat called Tom, and it sort of fitted.

That night I gave it some chopped-up chicken mixed with a bit of rice and Tom made quick work of it, spending quite a bit of time cleaning himself up afterwards. He stood by the back door and I let him out, where presumably he did his business in the yard and then waited patiently by the door for me to let him in again. Good, I thought, I won't have to get kitty litter; he seemed to be housetrained.

So we settled in together, Tom and I. He sat on my lap in the evenings and purred, and seemed to be happy. He was company. I didn't realise how much I needed company. I started to look forward to coming home from work. He stayed outside during the day, and ate just about anything I gave him.

I worked in an office as PA to an accountant. Not the most exciting of jobs. But it paid the rent.

'You should go out more often,' said Jan, one of the secretaries. 'Have some fun, get a life. How about coming over to my place for dinner on Saturday night? I'll invite Gerry,' she added with a bit of a smile.

Gerry was new to the office, middle-aged like me, and seemed a nice enough chap. I quite liked him. I was about to say, 'Thanks, OK, I'll come,' when a thought struck me. 'What about Tom?' I said. 'I don't usually go out in the evening. He might fret.'

'Who's Tom?' asked Jan.

'My cat,' I said.

'You've go to be joking!' exclaimed Jan. 'You're worried about your cat?'

Yes, well, it did seem a bit ridiculous, worrying about the cat, so I said I would go, and I did, and had a really nice time. Gerry and I seemed to hit it off, and I invited him back for dinner on the following Wednesday.

After I arrived home, quite late that Saturday night, I couldn't find Tom. I had left him inside with the TV going on low, just so that he would have some company. Then I found a pile of cat poo on the kitchen floor and scratch marks on the arm of my best armchair.

Realising I should have got a litter tray for when I was out and Tom was in, I didn't tell him off too much when I finally discovered him. He was in the bedroom. He had obviously been sleeping on my bed judging from the dent on my doona and not in his bed in the kitchen where he normally slept. I would have to remember to close the bedroom door. I let him out for a while before going to bed, and when he came back in, he went straight to his bed, completely ignoring me. Almost as if he was sulking, I thought. How odd.

Things got back to normal, and the following Wednesday I stopped at the shop on the way home from work for steaks and other stuff to make a nice dinner for Gerry, who was coming that evening. I was quite looking forward to it, and getting really annoyed with Tom, who somehow sensed something different was going on. He hung around me in the kitchen and kept getting under my feet.

'Go away, Tom,' I said, giving him a gentle push with my foot.

Immediately, he arched his back, swished his tail angrily and hissed at me. I was totally shocked. This was the first time Tom had shown any animosity towards me.

I opened the back door and pointed to the yard. 'Outside with you,' I said loudly. 'You can stay there until you can behave.'

He went out, but I felt a bit bad because it was starting to rain.

Half an hour later, Gerry arrived, and when I let him in Tom came in as well. He had managed to get over the side fence from the backyard and into the front, and was waiting under the porch by the front door.

Gerry looked around appreciatively. 'Nice place you have, Sue,' he smiled. 'Something smells good,' he added, as he handed me a bottle of wine.

Tom had made himself scarce, and I didn't think too much about him until we had finished dinner, and were sitting in the lounge having coffee. I was having a good time. The meal had turned out well and we were happily chatting.

Tom suddenly appeared in the doorway glowering. Which sounds like a silly thing to say about a cat, but that's what it seemed like.

He looked angry, his tail gently swishing, eyes fixed upon Gerry, who didn't realise the impact he was having.

'Oh, you have a cat,' he said. 'What's his name?'

'It's Tom.' I called him over. 'Come on, Tom,' I said, 'meet Gerry.'

Slowly, Tom walked across the room, eyes on Gerry, who reached out to stroke him. 'Hello, Tom.'

Big mistake, I realised too late. Tom arched his back, hissed and struck out with a paw, nails out, and quick as lightening scratched Gerry on the back of his hand.

He drew back with a cry of horror, raising his hand to his mouth. 'That's a vicious cat,' he shouted. 'How can you put up with that? Look at my hand!' – which was indeed oozing blood. He was angry and shocked, using bad language and, in my opinion, totally over-reacting.

'I'm so sorry.' I was distraught. 'Tom, you bad cat,' I yelled at him.

He disappeared into the kitchen, and I helped Gerry up and into the bathroom, where I ran the cold water tap on the scratch. It wasn't really that bad once the bleeding had stopped, and I had put some sticking plaster on it. But the night was spoiled and Gerry went home shortly afterwards, with a brief goodbye and still looking upset. A bit of a wuss, I thought. I probably won't be seeing him again.

So here we are, Tom on my lap purring away, TV on, nice and cosy. My brief attempt at wining and dining with the opposite sex had turned into a big disaster thanks to Tom. But then I had also seen a side of Gerry that I wouldn't have suspected. That was lucky.

So I pondered on the lucky or not status of black cats. It seems to me that it is the cat who decides whether it is going to be lucky or not. Humans have nothing to do with it.

Colours

The man stood on top of the bluff looking out to sea. In his hand, he had a piece of paper which he was reading. Then he folded it over, and stuffed it in his pants pocket. After a moment, he took it out again, reread it and then placed the note on the ground, half hiding it with a rock, so that it would be clearly visible to anyone walking by. He kicked off his shoes and placed them alongside the note, then, apparently changing his mind, he put them back on again. He walked to the edge of the cliff and stood, watching the people below.

Far beneath him on the beach, there were picnickers, surfers and sunbathers getting ready to pack up for the day. They had stopped momentarily to watch the sunset. The sky was slowly turning from the brilliant blue of a beautiful day to a darker purple right above.

The setting sun slowly dipping towards the horizon was a magnificent sight, turning from bright yellow to a radiant breathtaking orange; changing the surrounding clouds into such a glorious panorama of beauty it made you want to hold your breath and wish you could bottle it, to bring out on days when you needed some special colour in your life.

For long moments, the water became a spectacular reflection of the sky, giving the watchers a feeling almost like reverential awe and wonder at the glorious sight unfolding before them. Then slowly, the light dimmed until it was all gone, leaving behind an emerging clear night with a rising moon.

The man on the bluff had been gazing transfixed at the spectacle. Tears gathered in his eyes. He had long forgotten such beauty existed. He waited as the sky darkened and until he could no longer see anyone on the beach. Then he retrieved the note from under the rock, tore it into pieces then threw them over the cliff for the breeze to scatter.

By the light of the moon, the man slowly walked back down the path, his step steady and a new determination in his eyes as he made his way back to from whence he had come.

Jane's Dream

When Jane Butler was ten years old, she had a dream. She wanted to be famous. She wasn't quite sure what she would be famous for but thought she could be a film star, or perhaps a ballet dancer. Then again, there was always music. Jane liked music and thought she could be a concert pianist. She persuaded her mum to let her have piano lessons, and for a few months she did quite well, but the scales were boring, and the strict piano teacher, Miss Bloombury, soon realised that Jane was not prepared to put in the work. She didn't like practising, and the second-hand piano that Jane's dad had bought soon stood silent and dusty.

Jane decided she would be much better at dancing. She had dreams of being a prima donna ballerina and dancing *Swan Lake* at the theatre.

'You have to stick at it,' her mum, Shirley, had said. 'You can't expect to get good at something unless you practise. I am not going to pay for ballet lessons and shoes and everything unless you take it seriously.'

'I will, I promise,' said Jane.

So she had gone to ballet lessons and, true to her word, she did try. She had watched pictures of dancers and even a DVD of *Swan Lake*. But sadly, Jane had gained weight. She found it harder and harder to stand on her toes and one day her teacher rang Shirley with the sad news.

'I'm sorry,' she said, 'but Jane has absolutely no aptitude as a dancer. She has trouble staying on her toes and is quite unable to keep in time with the music. I really think you are wasting your money. Perhaps she has an aptitude for something else.'

Jane was secretly relieved. Ballet had been very hard and she wanted to stop but didn't have the heart to tell her parents and see their disappointed faces.

And so it went. Jane tried athletics and watched the Commonwealth games, admiring all the runners and swimmers. She took up swimming enthusiastically, soon realising, however, that she would never be able to swim fast enough to compete in competitions, In fact, getting up early every morning to go to practice was much too hard. Jane definitely was not a morning person.

In fact, when it came down to it, the only thing that she really enjoyed was reading. She realised that nobody ever got famous by reading and gradually Jane's dream of becoming famous one day didn't look like it was going to happen.

That year when she had been ten, Jane's mum had given her daughter a diary for Christmas. It was a beautiful leather-bound one with a page for every day. Jane loved it. On the first page she had written, 'One day I am going to be famous.'

Just before going to sleep, and after she had read at least one chapter of the book she was currently reading, Jane would write in her diary. When that first year had passed, she bought herself another one with her pocket money and wrote down everything that had happened during the day. There were descriptions of her friends, the scrapes her little brother got into. Later on, there were her descriptions of her pitiful attempts at trying to cook. (She had started watching *Master Chef*, thinking how easy it would be to be a famous chef.)

She started taking extra lessons in art. She had decided that it wouldn't be too hard to be a famous artist and brought home many offerings of her work that generally had remarks like 'Jane would probably benefit from having private lessons if she is to take art seriously.'

Jane didn't realise it but she had a great sense of humour. She could always laugh at herself and this was apparent from the little asides and notes sometimes written around the edges of the page when she wanted to include something she had forgotten.

'How is your diary coming along?' asked Shirley one day.

'Great, thanks, Mum,' Jane answered.

Jane knew her mum would be interested in what she had written, but she wasn't about to show her or anyone else. Not even her best friend Dora. For some reason, Jane decided that this was her own special thing which was to be shared with no one.

At the end of each year, she put the diary away in her bottom drawer, and with her pocket money bought another one at the newsagents for the following year.

As time passed, Jane eventually left school with average marks and found a job in a local bookshop, which pleased her immensely. She didn't have to do anything too active and she was surrounded by books.

Shirley never mentioned the diary again, assuming that like everything else it had been a nine-day wonder.

Everything that Jane couldn't talk about with anyone else went into the diary. She was short and a bit overweight. Her hair was nondescript and she didn't bother too much with make-up. Plus, her eyes were weak and she had started to wear reading glasses. She had never been asked out on a date. Jane thought that she seemed to be surrounded with tall, willowy, glamorous girls who were always going out to somewhere exciting. Most of the time it didn't bother her too much. But there were some times, she had to admit, when it would be nice to have someone to go out with, especially when she was invited to somewhere and they said bring a partner. So she usually didn't go.

But she kept her diaries going. As the years passed, they grew in number and gradually took up more space in the drawer, so Jane transferred them to a box which she slid under the bed.

When Jim Batts came into her life ,she had more or less decided that it was time she started looking for a place of her own She was twenty-five, single and still living with her parents.

Jim was one of her best customers in the bookshop. He was, she thought, a few years older than her, nondescript-looking, slightly built and beginning to go bald. He seemed quite shy, and scarcely said more to her than to ask if there was anything new in stock. She thought he must read an awful lot as he was always in the shop looking through the second-hand books at the back, which were much cheaper than the new ones.

When Jim finally got up the courage to ask Jane if she would do him the honour of dining with him one evening, she was quite amazed, and flattered, and unbelieving at first. But he had this old-fashioned courtesy with his manner which she found quite engaging. So it didn't take long for her to thank him for his invitation.

That night, the diary had quite of lot of thoughts written down that Jane couldn't possibly have spoken about. When the next evening Jim picked her up in a beautiful well kept Mercedes, she felt more excited than she had in years. Shirley stood at the door waving them off with a beaming smile.

After that first date there were many more. Jim had a small publishing business and they had plenty to talk about. Six months later they were married and Jane forgot all about her diaries. She didn't need to confide her thoughts to paper any more. She could talk to Jim. He listened, he advised, he never judged. He was, she thought, just perfect.

They put a deposit down on a small house and when moving day came Jane put the diaries with other boxes of things to be sorted out another time. So there they stayed.

It was a couple of years later that Jim had decided to clean out the spare room and came upon Jane's box of diaries. He took them into the kitchen, where she was preparing dinner. 'What about these, pet?' he asked. 'Do you want to keep them?' He pulled one of the books out. 'Oh, they're diaries,' he said. 'Can I read them?'

Jane smiled. 'I'd forgotten all about them,' she said. 'It's just a lot of childish scribbling. Another box for the garbage bin.' She glanced at him. 'You can read them if you like. Probably give you a bit of a laugh,' she added, and she turned back to the sink.

Jim sat down and was soon engrossed. Occasionally he laughed out loud. He looked up with an amazed expression on his face. 'Jane. Pet. These are pure gold. Do you know, you are an amazing writer.'

Jane laughed. 'Rubbish. They're just the ramblings of a mixed-up kid. I used to write all sorts of things down that I couldn't talk about with anyone else.'

'But that's just it. This is stuff that any kid or teenager would relate to.'

'Are you serious?' Jane looked askance. 'You really think so?'

'Yes.' He came and gave her a hug. 'I want to publish them.' He gave her a serious look. 'With your permission of course.'

Jane looked doubtful. 'Are you sure? Why would anyone want to read stuff like that?'

'You'd be surprised.' Jim was looking unusually animated. 'Are you sure you don't mind?'

Jane was very reluctant and thought hard for a moment. 'Well, okay.' She gave in. 'But you have to change the names, including mine. I couldn't bear it if someone recognised themselves, or me for that matter.'

So that was what happened. *Mary Jane's Diary* started to appear in a fairly new teenagers' publication. It had an immediate response. Emails, Facebook likes and tweets soon appeared in the social media. 'Who is Mary Jane?' they wanted to know. 'What happened next?' 'Did she become a ballerina?' They couldn't wait for the next instalment.

Jane's dream had come true. She had become famous. Anonymously, it is true, but famous is famous.

Jeremiah Johnson

Jeremiah Johnson had always envied his twin brother Jake's hair. It was black and curly, unlike his own, which was black and straight. Jake always had the girls hanging around him and had no trouble getting dates. He had a likeable free and easy manner, a big smile and never seemed to worry about anything.

Jeremiah, on the other hand, had a nasty little streak that made him want to knock the smile off his brother's face. He was jealous of Jake's looks and his apparent good luck, especially with girls. Jeremiah couldn't understand why. He actually had bigger muscles than his brother, he was a snappy dresser and always tried to be a gentleman. He tried to look happy, even when he wasn't, which was quite a bit of the time because he was so busy comparing himself to his brother.

Jeremiah decided it must be because of his hair. No matter how he tried to style it with gel or had a trendy cut, it wasn't as good as if it were curly. So one day he made a big decision. Without telling anyone, he made an appointment at a unisex hairdresser in the next suburb to have a perm.

'Just make it curly,' he said to the gay hairdresser who was flapping around exclaiming how 'Sir will be enchanted with the result.'

Jeremiah prayed that no one he knew would come into the salon, and two hours later after much mirror gazing, admiring himself, and paying an exorbitant price with money saved from his part-time after-school job, he jumped on his bike and pedalled home.

'What have you done with your hair?' His mother was gazing at him wide-eyed. 'You look like Jake.'

'Oh Bro,' said his brother, 'what have you done? Your hair was fine as it was. In fact, I was thinking of getting mine straightened. Curly hair is going out of fashion.'

Jeremiah said nothing. Yeah, you would say that, he thought. Now you have some real competition. Now you won't be so superior.

Saturday they had both been invited to a birthday barbecue in a neighbour's backyard. Jeremiah could hardly wait. He dressed with care, flexed his muscles, carefully combed his new curly locks and practised smiling in the bathroom mirror.

It was a good party. Jake as usual was sitting on the garden seat with a girl on either side of him. Jeremiah, alas, was sitting by himself over by the outside bar with a plate of food on his lap. The girls had taken no more notice of him than before. No one had commented on his hair except for Julie, one of the neighbours, who had earlier tapped him on the shoulder, but then jumped back with a start when he turned round.

'Oh, sorry,' she said. 'I thought you were Jake.' She peered at him. 'You should have left your hair straight. It was easier to tell the difference.'

Jeremiah was left looking at a neat little butt in a tight red miniskirt as she tottered away in search of his brother.

Metamorphosis

Once upon a time there was a small boy called Alexander.

Alexander was nine years old, with red hair and freckles. Everyone called him Alex. The only time he was called Alexander was by his mother, when he had done something bad and then it was 'Alexander, what do you have to say for yourself?'

Usually he had nothing to say for himself because he could never think of a reason for some of the things he did. Like teasing his sister, or hiding the cat in the wardrobe, or sneaking his vegetables to the dog under the table. Or other inventive things done on the spur of the moment because it seemed to be a good idea at the time.

Alex always seemed to be in trouble, even when things happened that were totally out of his control. Like when the next-door neighbour, who was visiting, slipped on the kitchen floor and broke her wrist. It wasn't his fault that his toast had slipped out of his hand and landed butter side down. He had quickly picked it up and eaten it before his mother saw him, leaving a blob of butter on the floor. Next-doors should have been looking where she was walking, he thought. And it wasn't his fault that his father's mobile phone had gone missing and was eventually found in the dog's bed. He got the blame for that, just because he had been playing go find with the dog.

Sometimes he wished he could have another name. Like Peter. Peter wouldn't get into trouble. Peter sounded like someone who would be appreciated for his brilliant ideas. And not made to feel guilty all the time. Maybe his mother would sometimes say, 'What a good boy you are, Peter.' That would be good.

So he decided to change his name. 'In future, my name will be Peter,' he announced one dinner time when all the family were there.

'What ever for?' His mum was surprised. 'What's wrong with Alex?' she asked.

'Don't be ridiculous,' said his father.

'Why do you want to be called Peter?' asked his sister, Katy. 'Is this another one of your stupid ideas?'

'I just do.' Alex was adamant. 'I don't like Alex any more. I want to be called Peter.'

So just to humour him, and because he actually had a really nice family who had been putting up with his weird and strange ways for a long time, they decided to humour him.

'OK,' said his mother. 'So eat your dinner, Peter.'

And Peter did. He ate all his greens without a fuss. Afterwards, when his mum asked him to help with the washing up, to her great surprise Peter agreed, without the groan of misery he usually made when asked to help with the chores.

Peter started doing his homework without being nagged, and when a bad thought crossed his mind like hiding Katy's best shoes in the pantry just for the pleasure of seeing her running around the house in a panic, he remembered he was not Alex any more. He had a bit of a tussle in his head for a few minutes while he wrestled with the problem, and almost forgot about Peter, but then he realised his family would laugh and talk about nine-day wonders. So he became Peter again and resisted temptation.

'It's like he's morphed into a different person,' remarked Katy one day. 'It's like a miracle.'

He told his teacher at school that his real name was Peter and not Alexander, and that his parents had made a mistake on his birth certificate. The teacher rang his mother to ask about this, who explained with embarrassment that there had been a mix-up and that it would be all right to call her son Peter in future. His teacher was very pleased to be receiving regular homework on time and, generally speaking, much improved on Alex's previous ad hoc presentations. So she didn't take the matter any further.

Peter's schoolmates were a bit bemused but soon decided that it was just Alex having a laugh, and thought it was a great joke.

Peter was becoming so good that he always had his hand up when the teacher asked for answers in class. His marks improved, but instead of the popular larrikin who was always up to mischief that his mates related to, they soon decided that he was no fun any more.

'I liked you better when you were Alex,' said his mate Jack. 'What did you have to go and change your name for?'

Peter's family at first were puzzled by this unexpectedly good behaviour. While it was quiet and peaceful at home, they missed the old boisterous Alex.

When his mum said one day, after he had helped bring in the washing, 'What a good boy you are, Peter,' it was surprisingly with a small hint of regret in her tone. Although it must be said that Peter's breast seemed to swell with pride at the unaccustomed praise.

Sometimes Alex emerged. Like the time he persuaded all his class mates to bring an apple for Miss Brown, their teacher, on the same day, and she ended up with twenty-five apples rolling around on her desk. Everyone thought it was a hoot and that the old Alex was back.

'This is very nice of you all,' she said somewhat warily. She looked accusingly for a moment at Peter as though she had a good idea who was responsible. Then shook her head. No, it couldn't be Peter, could it, he had been so good lately. She put her suspicions to one side and all the apples were distributed at lunchtime.

Peter was a smart boy. He had by now realised that if Alex decided to do something a bit inventive and tricky, Peter wouldn't be blamed. Now that he was Peter the Good, he could get away with anything. But the truth was that he was becoming bored with being good. He kept getting these brilliant ideas for a good trick, and it was getting harder and harder to remember whether he was Alex the Bad or Peter the Good.

It all came crashing down around him one day when Alex decided it would be a good idea to sneak a fake spider into Katy's bed and waited for the satisfying screams that would come when she discovered it.

Unfortunately, this time no one was fooled.

'What have you got to say for yourself, Peter?' asked his mum with the sternest tone he had heard for a long time.

'It wasn't me, it was Al…' he started to say, and then realised that this time it wouldn't work.

'Apologise to Katy.' His mum was really cross. 'You gave her a big fright. You know she's scared of spiders.'

Peter gave a huge sigh. 'I'm sorry,' he said.

Katy gave him a little push. 'Just you wait, ALEX,' she said. 'I'll get you back.'

They both quickly disappeared with whoops of laughter and suddenly things were back to normal.

That was that really. Afterwards, Peter the Good emerged occasionally, but only on special occasions when it was really important to make a good impression for some reason or another, but generally speaking Alex was back.

Much to everyone's relief, orderly chaos was restored.

Night Visitor

'Someone's at the door.' Joe sat up in bed with a start. 'Who could it be at this time of night?'

'Goodness knows.' Gladys wasn't impressed. She had been about to drop off to sleep. 'You'd better go and see. It might be someone in trouble.'

'It might be a burglar.'

'If it was a burglar, they wouldn't be knocking on the door.'

'They would if they had a gun.'

'Well, we have nothing to steal, and we haven't any money.'

Joe wasn't too keen. 'It's a really dark and stormy night. Nobody in their right mind would be out on a night like this.'

'Well, go and open the door and find out.'

'I think I'll have a look through the window first. Just to see if I can see who it is.'

'Joe, for goodness sake… Well, can you see anything?'

Joe was straining his head to see around the side. 'I can see a very tall person in what looks like armour. I think it's that toffee-nosed knight from next door. He looks a bit agitated.'

Gladys couldn't resist. 'You were probably right then. It is a dark and stormy knight.'

'Very funny!' Joe shook his head. 'I wonder what his problem is. Since he's been made a knight, it has really gone to his head. He's never even given us the time of day, nor has his fancy-looking wife, and now he comes banging on the door at midnight.'

'You could always go and find out what he wants.'

'OK. I'll go and see.' Joe put on his dressing gown and made his way to the front door.

What appeared to be someone with chainmail armour on was stamping irritably on the doorstep.

Suppressing a snigger, Joe managed, 'Good evening, Sir Jeremy. How are you?'

'I'm well, but I'm having a problem removing my armour.'

'Why are you wearing armour?'

'It was for a knight's dinner. All the Sirs and Madams had to dress up, so I wore my armour, but I can't get it off. Even my wife can't get it off. It seems to have stuck. So can you get it off?'

'Well, I don't know. What's it worth?'

'What do you mean, what's it worth? I just want you to get the damn thing off.'

'What's the magic word?'

'What are you talking about?' Sir Jeremy shouted. 'What magic word? Are you nuts?'

'You could ask nicely.' Joe was enjoying himself.

'OK, I'm asking nicely. I suppose you expect me to say please. OK. Please. Now get it off. There's a bolt around the back which seems to have tightened and I can't reach it properly.'

'Did you have a nice dinner?'

'Yes, very nice. Why are you asking about dinner? Just get this thing off.'

'We didn't have any dinner,' said Gladys, who had got up from bed and intrigued by the conversation had decided to go and see what was happening.

'Well, that's not my concern. Now have you got some pliers or something?'

'I don't know. I'll have to go out to the toolshed and have a look.' Joe decided to take his time and milk this for all it was worth.

'Well, hurry up. I don't have all night to hang around here.' Sir Jeremy looked up at the dark sky. 'I need to get home.'

'My wife and I were in bed and it's a very cold outside. I think you'd better come back in the morning.'

'Don't be ridiculous. Look here, it's started raining. At least you could let me come in.'

'OK, you can come in.'

'Thank you.' He clomped in rattling his armour. 'Well?' he shouted.

'Well what?'

'Are you going to get this thing off me or not?'

'I'm thinking about it.'

'Look, um…what's your name?'

'Joe. Joe Packham, and this is my wife Gladys.'

'Yes, well…look, Joe, I'm er sorry to disturb you, but if you would help get this thing off me I would appreciate it.' He had lowered his voice ,which had turned into a very slightly pleading tone.

'We've been living next door for ten years.' Joe wasn't prepared to cut any slack just yet.

'So?'

'So this is the first time you have ever spoken to us.'

'Yes, well, I'm sure that's unfortunate. I'll get my wife to call tomorrow. Now just get this armour off.'

Joe waited.

Sir Jeremy glared for a minute. Then, 'Please,' he managed to say.

'My Gladys went to call on your wife when you first moved in and she pretended to be out, but she wasn't out, she was peeping through the curtain. Isn't that right, Gladys?'

'Yes, Joe, and I thought it was very rude.'

'Well, I'm sure that was unfortunate. Sometimes my wife has bad headaches and can't see anyone. Now I need to get home. My wife will be wondering where I am.'

At that moment, the visor in front of the helmet he was wearing dropped down over his face, which was getting redder by the minute.

He pushed it back up. 'Now are you going to get some tools or what?' he shouted. The pleading tone had disappeared and he was beginning to sound desperate.

Joe looked at Gladys. 'What do you think, pet?'

'Well, it is a bit cold and I would like to go back to bed.' Gladys was shivering.

'OK.' He went over to the kitchen drawer, from which he pulled out a small bag of tools. He took out a screwdriver. 'Turn round,' he said.

With a grunt, the knight turned round and, after a long look at the back of the strange outfit, Joe quickly removed two small screws, and suddenly the armour appeared to fall to pieces. It dropped to the floor with a clatter, leaving the defrocked knight standing in his underwear and still wearing the helmet.

Joe and Gladys couldn't stop themselves. They laughed and laughed. Sir Jeremy picked up all the bits and pieces, pulled the visor back down, hiding his face, which was now a bright red. He hurried as fast as he could back to the front door, which Joe opened for him with a flourish and a bow.

'Good knight,' he said.

UFO

'Come quick. There's a flying saucer,' the boy's voice rang out. He was calling his brother, who was playing on the swing in the back garden.

They were soon both pointing to the sky with great excitement. Their mother, who wondered what they were shouting about, quickly came to see what was causing all the fuss. She took one look at the sky and at once phoned her neighbour, who also came out and joined them in the backyard.

They all looked in amazement at the object flying overhead. It looked like all the pictures they had ever seen of flying saucers. Round, like a squashed balloon with a knob on top and windows all around the side. It shone and glittered as it slowly revolved and hovered overhead. It was evening and the failing light made it difficult to see much detail. The setting sun threw an eerie glow onto the UFO hanging in a nearly clear sky, with just a few light clouds scudding about in the slight breeze.

Suddenly the object dipped and quickly disappeared behind the stand of tall gums alongside the track bordering the paddock across the road. By now, other people had seen the object. Phones had been busy and there were quite a few people were starting to arrive. Someone opened the gate to the paddock, not worrying about the cows quietly grazing, and everyone rushed through.

'It's gone,' someone cried out.

But no, suddenly it appeared again from behind the trees on the other side of the paddock, quickly rising high and then higher and higher, where it seemed to hover.

A police car screamed to a halt out on the road and the sirens of an ambulance could be heard in the distance. More and more people arrived, seemingly from nowhere. Social media were working overtime and word had passed around in an amazingly short time. Cameras were produced. Excitement reigned and people were talking animatedly about what to do if it landed.

'Suppose they want to know who our leader is?' some bright spark shouted.

People watching television saw a newsflash. 'Breaking news,' it said. 'Reports have come in of a UFO sighting over a paddock in outback Wooliginigup.'

Suddenly there was someone shouting on a megaphone. It was a policeman. 'Everybody get back,' he yelled. 'Clear the paddock.'

No one moved. A couple of big trucks drew to a halt, and soldiers in full combat gear, rifles at the ready, descended onto the now churned-up ground. A TV news helicopter had been dispatched and was on its way.

There was a hush now, the air filled with apprehension. Suddenly it became serious business. They all watched in awe as the object descended, slowly at first, then with amazing speed disappeared again behind the trees over in the next paddock. For a few long minutes, they waited for it to appear again, but nothing happened. It seemed to have gone.

At a shouted command, the soldiers, with rifles at the ready, proceeded with a quick trot over the paddock to the stand of trees on the other side, some of them occasionally stumbling as they stepped in a pothole or a pile of cow dung. Some of the braver civilians started to follow, but the policeman with the megaphone shouted a warning to keep back or they would be charged with obstruction.

Over in the far paddock, two young blokes were busily gathering up the enormous kite they had painstakingly constructed in their shed. It was as big as a mini car and was beautifully painted. They let the balloon-like structure down, and tidied up the long pieces of string which had been attached in various places.

'That was awesome,' said one, as they carefully stowed it all away in the back of their ute. 'It works a treat. I think we have a good chance of a trophy at the next kite-flying comp. We'll have to keep it a secret, though. We don't want anyone else nicking our ideas.'

'Hey, listen,' said the other one. 'Hear that?' He looked through the trees. 'Hurry,' he said, 'let's get out of here. It looks like the army. It may be a military exercise or something. I think we may be trespassing.'

So they quickly departed, over a backtrack, away from the main road.

When the soldiers arrived, some puffing with the unexpected exercise, not a trace was left. Just some tyre tracks, if anyone had bothered to look. But no one did. In any case, by then it was dark and the moon was rising.

Most people were quite disappointed when they discovered the UFO had gone. Some said it was a hoax, some put it down to mass hysteria, but those who were there knew it was true. They were there. They had pictures of it on their cameras. So they had proof, didn't they?

Patch

'Did you get one of these?' The long-haired tattooed youth was standing outside the school hall, handing out election pamphlets.

'No thanks,' I said. 'I don't need one. I know who I'm going to vote for.'

He shoved the notice at me. 'Would you please read this,' he said.

'Why?' I didn't look at it and started to move away. 'I told you, I know who I'm going to vote for.'

He moved in front of me, invading my personal space. I was getting annoyed and tried to sidestep but he persisted, holding his pamphlet up again.

'Please,' he said. 'I would really like you to have a read of this. It's important.'

I didn't want any further confrontation and so, to get out of his way, and with a big sigh of annoyance, I took the leaflet and stuffed it into my pocket.

The boy moved out of my way. 'Thank you,' he said surprisingly, as I passed, then he looked behind me, ready for the next unsuspecting person coming along to vote.

I finally got inside the building, and went over to the table, behind which people were sitting, ready to tick off names and hand out voting forms. So I got signed in, collected two forms and then had to queue for a booth before I could complete the voting papers and put the ticks in the right places.

While I was waiting for my turn, I remembered the leaflet the young man had insisted I read, and I pulled it out of my pocket, intending to throw it in one of the garbage bins they had around the place. I gave it a quick glance and was about to screw it up, when the heading on the leaflet caught my eye. I realised it was nothing to do with voting, so I started to read it.

'LOST. A SHAGGY DOG WHICH GOES BY THE NAME OF PATCH.' It went on to describe a black and white mutt of no particular breed, which had disappeared from the owner's garden in the vicinity of the school where we were at the moment. There was a phone number and the owner's name, Harry.

Well, I had to admit, he had a good idea. It was after all, voting day and plenty of people around. I felt bad for my rudeness to the young man, who after all was only looking for his lost dog. It was quite enterprising of him to take advantage of the opportunity presented to him that day. So after the voting was done and I was walking home, I kept an eye out for any stray-looking black and white dog which answered to the name of Patch. But I saw nothing. There was a shaggy brown dog in a front yard, and I saw a couple of cats, but nothing else.

Later that day I thought about the young man and whether he had found his dog, and as I had to go out to go to the shops, I drove home the long way round, carefully scanning each street for a black and white dog.

Suddenly I braked. There he was, a shaggy black and white dog in a front yard, standing by the gate and looking out at my car. He seemed so sad. I looked to see if there appeared to be anyone home. There was no car in the driveway, the garage door was open and empty.

Apprehensively, I slowly climbed out of the car the approached the gate. 'Hello,' I said. I reached through the bars to give the dog a stroke and he licked my hand. 'I wonder if your name is Patch,' I said.

His ears perked up and his tail wagged and my heart did a flip. He excitedly started to jump up the gate, but it was too high for him to jump over.

This is him for sure, I decided. This is Patch. I looked around to see if anyone had noticed, but there was no one in sight, no pedestrians or parked cars. The coast was clear. So I quietly opened the gate and Patch walked through and made straight for the car. I opened the rear door and he jumped in. It was as easy as that. I drove away quickly, putting my seatbelt on as I went. I couldn't believe what I had just done. This was totally out of character. I'd never done such an impulsive thing in my life before.

We were home within ten minutes and I couldn't wait to phone Harry.

'Hello,' he said, and I recognised the young man's voice.

'Hello,' I replied. 'Er, this is Emily Johnson. It's about your dog.'

'Oh,' he said. 'What about my dog?'

'Well, I've found him.' There was a silence. I thought that he must be too overwhelmed to speak. 'He's fine,' I said in my best reassuring voice. 'You don't have to worry, I'll look after him till you can come and get him.'

There was another silence. Then Harry said. 'Um, I've got my dog. Someone found him yesterday and brought him back. You must have found another dog.'

'Oh,' was all I could manage.

'If you've found another lost dog, you could take him to the dog kennels and they'll find him another home,' Harry said helpfully.

A worrying thought was now going through my head. 'How did you lose your dog?' I said next.

'Someone must have opened the gate and let him out.' Harry sounded indignant. 'Some people just don't think about closing the gate. I have to go now. Thanks for calling. Goodbye.' And then he hung up.

An uncomfortable feeling of dread was invading my being, and after ten minutes thinking about what I had done, I realised there was no alternative. I put the dog back in the car and drove around to the same street again. I had to look for the right place. I was in such a hurry to get away before, I didn't take note of the house number. Standing at the gate was a worried looking lady who seemed mightily relieved when I opened the door and Patch jumped out of the car, his tail wagging madly as he rushed to greet her.

'Oh, thank goodness,' she said. 'Thank you so much. Someone must have let him out of the gate. Harry would have been so upset if he'd got lost again.' She peered closely at me. 'How did you know where he lived. Where did you find him?'

'Just up the street,' I said. 'A neighbour recognised him and told me where you lived. I have to go,' I added, then quickly got back into the car, waved goodbye and took off feeling, I must admit, a little bit stupid.

When It All Went Down the Toilet

Joe Collins was a small-time crook. He specialised in break and enter, and targeted homes when the owners were away all day at work. He always entered the premises where the best opportunity presented itself. Sometimes through an unlocked door, or maybe a half-opened window. He looked for small, easily hidden objects like jewellery, or cash. He wasn't interested in drugs, that was too risky; he wanted something he could easily dispose of or spend. In his opinion, he wasn't greedy.

Joe had a criminal record. Ten years ago, he had been caught stealing a jumper from a shop. He had gone to court and pleaded guilty. He had been fined and his fingerprints had been taken. So Joe was very careful. He always wore gloves and never left any trace of himself. He always left everything the way he had found it, and sometimes, unless there was an obviously broken window, the owners wouldn't know he had paid them a visit until they noticed something missing.

Bert Barker was a policeman who specialised in forensics. He was the ultimate fingerprint copper who took great pride in his work. Everybody leaves prints somewhere, he would say, and even if the crook wasn't on the main database, he would get caught eventually. Which was why Bert was particularly frustrated with the culprit who was continuing to evade capture after a series of break and enters on his patch.

Bert had a good idea who it was, due to bits of information here and there, and one particularly good description from an elderly lady who maintained that she saw a man in a hoodie sneaking around to the back of the next-door house. She had rung 000 like a good citizen but by the time the police had arrived he was long gone. When the owners arrived home, they discovered that a pearl necklace had been stolen. Once again, Bert had meticulously checked the house for fingerprints and any other forensic material, but as usual came up blank.

Joe had decided that it was time he moved on. He had done this neighbourhood. This was to be his last job. He had sussed out the house and knew the owners were away all day. It had plenty of bushes around the front and was not very visible from the street.

He walked in the gate and around to the back, where he found a laundry window open a bit at the bottom. Piece of cake, he thought. He put his gloves on then eased the fly screen off, and gently pushed the window up. Then heaving himself up, he crawled through the window, jumped down and proceeded to wander through the house.

'Aha,' he muttered. He had spotted a nice little gold watch sitting on the bedside table. He stuffed it in his pocket and looked around for some cash, but no luck this time. He wandered into the kitchen and opened the fridge door, where he spotted a carton of orange juice. He took it out and had a good swig before returning it. Mustn't be greedy, he thought.

Suddenly Joe felt a sudden need to go to the toilet and decided that he might as well use the one here. He took the gloves off, stuffing them into his pocket while he did the business, then put them back on before leaving and pulling the window down to the exact same position it was in when he entered. Then he carefully replaced the flyscreen.

It was only when he had got back home and was sitting down in front of the telly with his dinner that he started thinking about the house he had done over that day. He had been worrying about leaving evidence in the loo, and made sure he flushed the toilet, but with a sinking heart now remembered he hadn't put his gloves back on again till afterwards. He wondered if that copper would think to look for fingerprints on the top of the toilet cistern. Joe decided to take no chances.

Early next morning, he was hurriedly loading his possessions into the back of his van when he saw the police car swinging around the corner and stopping right behind him.

Bert Barker had a big smile on his face as he quickly got out of the vehicle dangling handcuffs. 'You're nicked,' he said. 'Face the car. Hands behind your back.'

With a sigh of resignation, Joe stuck his hands out behind him and Bert snapped the handcuffs on. 'You'd better lock up your van,' he told him. 'You won't be travelling anywhere any time soon.'

'It was the prunes wot did it,' Joe muttered bitterly. 'If it wasn't for them prunes, I wouldn't have had to go, would I?'

'Well, you won't have to worry about prunes for a bit. Not where you're going.' Bert was probably the happiest policeman on the beat that day as he prodded Joe into the back of the police car. 'Mind your head,' he said kindly.

All About Slamming Doors

The door slammed in his face.

Furiously he pounded on it. 'Let me in,' he yelled, 'let me in. You can't do this to me.'

There was no sound from inside and his pleas went unanswered.

He started to sob, his cries becoming louder. 'This isn't fair, you haven't given me a chance,' he shouted. 'What did I do to deserve this?'

He realised he was getting out of control, so he tried to calm himself down, realising that he had to try a new tactic if he was going to get her to open the door. 'Please, come on, open the door, don't be like this.' He began to cajole, trying to sound calm and stop the hysterical sound his voice had been making.

Still there was silence. He quietened down and tried to hear what was going on inside. There was no keyhole so he couldn't even have a peek.

Again the anger surged and he punched the door with his fists. 'Open this door,' he shouted, 'or I promise you'll be sorry.'

Still there was no response.

Slowly he slid down the wall outside and sat on the floor, frustrated and furious.

After a few moments, he began to think logically. If she assumes I've gone away, he thought, she'll open the door to have a look, and then I'll be able to surprise her and get back inside. Then maybe we can talk about this, and she'll see how unfair she's being.

Stamping his feet a little, he walked away from the door, then very quietly crept back and leant up against it. He listened, ear pressed against the door. He could faintly the humming of a motor running. What is she doing now? he wondered. How long before she comes out? She has to come out sometime.

So he quietly waited. His anger calmed now that he had a plan. He was getting cramp, standing still and tensed for so long, so he sat down again, resting his back against the door.

He looked at his watch. Another five minutes had passed.

Without warning, the door suddenly opened, and he fell backwards into the room. He tried to stand up and hold onto the door at the same time, to stop her closing it again.

She looked angry. 'What do you think you're doing?' she shouted. 'Can't you be patient for once. You really are an absolute pain.' She picked up a damp towel and chucked it at him. 'There you are,' she said, 'the bathroom's all yours, and make sure you clean up afterwards.'

She left, and the door slammed in his face.

The Scarecrow

The scarecrow stood alone in the middle of the paddock. He was on duty, a sentry guarding his kingdom of corn almost ready to be picked. A somewhat menacing figure over six feet tall, constructed with straw, bits of wood and tatty clothes. He wore an old patchwork shirt, jeans with holes and ragged edges, and a belt holding up the pants with a big metal buckle in the front. A pair of boots with soles hanging off were attached to the straw legs, and an old akubra hat had bits of string and corks dangling from the brim.

But the most frightening part of him was his face. A dirty-looking white ball with bits of straw stuck around the edges. A face had been painted on by someone with macabre tendencies. The eyes were black, drooping down at the ends, giving a sad appearance. A nose had been attached – a red clown's nose supported with string tied around the back. But the mouth was the most scary. Like something out of a horror story. Red, gaping, with pointy teeth, and the red paint had run in places, giving the appearance of dripping blood, ready to take a bite out of anyone who was brave enough to get too close.

At least that was what young Jim thought. He lived at the farm on the other side of the wood which bordered the cornfield.

'You are not to go into the cornfield,' his father had told him. 'It's dangerous.'

'Why is it dangerous?' asked Jim.'

'It just is,' said his dad, Tom. 'The old fella who owns that field is a little bit – er – peculiar, he's very particular about who goes on his property. He doesn't take kindly to trespassers.'

This of course was like a red rag to a bull. Jim, being a normal ten-year-old, who until now had always done more or less as he was told, was feeling adventurous, and being told not to go somewhere because it was dangerous was just asking for an investigation. After all, it was only a cornfield, wasn't it? So young Jim had decided to investigate, which was why he was now standing in front of the scarecrow.

He walked around it, touching the straw extending from the ends of the outstretched arms. He had recoiled slightly when he first saw the face, then told himself not to be a wuss. It was just a stupid scarecrow. It might scare the birds, but it certainly didn't scare him.

Then, out of the corner of his eye, he saw one of the boots move. At first he thought he had accidentally knocked it when walking around, even though he couldn't actually recall doing that. When he looked again, the boot was stock still. He walked around again noticing how a pole stuck into the ground was supporting the scarecrow to stop it falling over.

He poked the back of the shirt, which felt quite solid, then he reached up and tipped the hat forward, so that it nearly came down over the eyes. He smiled to himself. This was really cool. He wouldn't mind having a go at making a scarecrow like this. His dad would probably be pleased. He could put it in the vegie patch.

Just then the leg moved forward, just a few centimetres, and then back again. This time Jim really saw it move. He hadn't touched it. He looked skywards; there was no wind. He stepped back a bit and squinted. It was a very bright day; maybe it was a trick of the light. Maybe he was imagining things and what he thought he saw happen didn't actually happen.

He moved a back a little way and squatted on the ground, his eyes fixed on the scarecrow's boots. Then he watched and waited. He waited about ten minutes, but nothing else happened. He was tiring of this and, deciding his imagination was working overtime, Jim checked the new watch his dad had given him for his tenth birthday. It was nearly teatime; his mum would be wondering where he was. So he got up and walked to the scarecrow once more for a last look before leaving. He reached forward to touch the belt buckle, and the right leg on the scarecrow suddenly moved with a jerk. Iit kicked up and the boot caught Jim right on the shin. It caught him unawares, and he fell backwards with a mighty yell.

Absolute horror engulfed his being as he sat for a moment

completely paralysed with fear. He looked up at the hideous face, which was now swivelling from side to side. He was painfully aware of the fact that his shin was hurting and his heart thumping.

Suddenly galvanised into action, Jim scrambled to his feet and started to run. He ran the fastest he had ever run in his life. He didn't look back until he reached the stile at the edge of the cornfield. He stopped for a moment to catch his breath, and then climbed over the fence to safety on the other side before he dared to look behind him. The scarecrow was in his usual place, immobile. Like nothing had happened at all.

Jim followed the path through the wood which led to his home. His shin was sore and there was an abrasion that was bleeding a bit.

'There you are, Jim,' his mum remarked. 'I was beginning to wonder where you were. Tea's just about ready.' She noticed he was limping a bit. 'What have you done? You're limping and you're bleeding. Oh, and look at your shorts, filthy!' She shook her head and sighed. 'You'd better go and clean up. Dad'll be home in a minute. And,' she warned, 'he'll want to know what you've been up to.'

Jim couldn't speak. How, he thought, could he say, 'The scarecrow kicked me,' especially when he wasn't supposed to be in the cornfield anyway. Who would believe him? He changed his shorts and put a band-aid on his leg, and hoped there wouldn't be any questions asked. Luckily, there weren't. His dad had other things on his mind and young Jim's grazed leg wasn't important enough to worry about.

Over in the farmhouse the other side of the paddock, Wally Simpson was sitting in front of his CCTV screen. He had cameras set up in various places around his precious cornfield and a very tiny camera fixed discreetly into the buckle of his scarecrow's belt. There was also one in the brim of the hat. Wally gave an evil chuckle as he pushed a button and watched as a remote control device lifted one leg of the scarecrow, and then the other one. It had worked well. Two other buttons controlled the arms, which could move up and down, and the head could swivel from side to side.

'That'll teach that little beggar,' he muttered. 'He won't be coming here again.'

He was right about that.

The Audition

Jeremy had been rehearsing for weeks. At first it seemed like he had a very long time to practise. It was just a dream, something that would happen in the future, but suddenly the day had arrived, it had become real, and in a few minutes it was all going to happen. His mother had driven him to the venue where the auditions were to be held. He had dressed in his best clothes – not too fancy, but neat and comfortable, they had said. So he was wearing his new jeans and a matching blue T-shirt which loosely covered his tummy.

Then he was waiting in the wings for his turn to go on, and a nice smiley young lady had put her arm around him.

'Don't be scared,' she whispered. 'You're going to be just fine.'

When they had the rehearsal that afternoon, they had told him not to worry about the lights, just fix your eyes on someone and pretend they are the only ones looking at you. He knew his mum would be near the front so he had decided he would just look for her and pretend to be in the lounge room at home.

Jeremy anxiously pushed his spectacles up onto his nose. He was getting sweaty and they kept slipping down. He looked down at his shoes to make sure the laces were still tied up properly. He imagined tripping up as he walked onto the stage and he started to shake. He wasn't going to be able to do it. He was going to chicken out.

But then they called his name. 'Next is Jeremy Baker,' the man on the stage shouted. 'Come on, Jeremy.'

The smiley lady gave him a gentle push. 'Off you go, pet,' she said. 'Best of luck.'

Suddenly he was there on the stage. The lights were so bright he could barely see. Then he spotted his mum, right there in the front row just to one side of the three judges. So Jeremy pushed his glasses back up, stood up straight and took hold of the microphone. He knew when to come in, he had practised it so many times. He closed his eyes for a moment, took a deep breath and waited for the music to start.

The first notes were a little bit wobbly, but all at once it was OK. He sang his song the best he knew how. He remembered everything his teacher had told him. When to breathe and how to hold the high note. His voice was high and clear with perfect pitch, the song soared and seemed to take on a life of its own, until the very last note. He had forgotten the huge audience watching and when the song finished, he felt as though he had been to another place. It was all a bit surreal, like a dream. But he felt good. He had done it. He looked at his mum, who was smiling happily.

Jeremy suddenly realised everyone had gone quiet, and wondered if he should just go off the stage. He stumbled a bit as he turned to go, but suddenly the audience erupted with cheers, whistles and claps. He looked amazed as people were getting up onto on their feet. He looked around the stage, but there was nobody else there. Were they cheering for him? Even the judges were standing up and the lady judge with the blonde hair looked as though she was crying.

The compère walked onto the stage with a big smile on his face. He looked down at the small unremarkable-looking ten-year-old boy who was now looking anxiously at the judges. He put his arm around him and gave him a little hug. 'Well done, Jeremy,' he said. 'That was totally awesome. Look,' he added, 'you've got three yeses.'

Above the judges' heads, in big golden lights were three exes.

Jeremy blinked and his anxious face changed into a big beam of pure joy. He raised one fist into the air and did a little twirl, then he had to stoop down to retie a shoelace.

The Water Bottle

Nina sat by the beach watching the sunset fill the sky with a golden glow. She felt restless, depressed, aware of seeming to be the only person by herself on the beach. There were family groups, and couples cuddling on the sand and children playing with balls and frisbies.

She sighed, and squinted into the sunset. Something had caught her eye. The tide was coming in bringing seaweed, and floating amongst it was something that looked like a water bottle. The swirling foam swished forward with an unexpected rush, reaching almost to her feet. That last wave had came in so fast it had almost caught her, then it receded again, leaving the bottle behind, stuck in the sand. It appeared to be a regular plastic water bottle with the label missing.

Nina got down from the rock she had been sitting on, then retrieved the bottle from the pile of seaweed. Normally she would have just disregarded it as rubbish, even though her conscience would have been nagging at her, knowing she should find a rubbish bin. Anyway, on this occasion she picked it up because she could see there was something inside.

Intrigued now, she peered closely at what appeared to be a piece of paper. It was folded over so she couldn't see what was written on it, or indeed if anything was. She unscrewed the lid and shook the bottle, trying to make the paper slide down, but of course it wouldn't. It must have been squeezed up to get it in there in the first place. There was no way it would come back out through the opening.

She debated for a moment – throw it back, look for a bin? – but only for a moment, because now she wanted to know if there was a written message inside. So she shook the sand off and tucked the bottle into her bag. then made her way home.

Nina lived by herself in a small house, walking distance from the beach. Most of the time she didn't mind being alone; there was always something to do, she had a part-time job she enjoyed, and she could walk on the beach whenever she felt like it. Generally speaking, she should have been quite content, but her life was predictable, regulated, uneventful, boring, and recently, like today, more and more she felt unsettled, unhappy. She wished something interesting would happen. She didn't know what exactly. Something, anything to cheer her up a bit.

At least, she thought now, this was slightly interesting. Nina looked at the bottle, wondering how best to get the paper out. If it had been glass, she could have broken it. She went out into the shed, where there were a few tools, still there since Jack had passed away a year ago. She found a small saw, and took it inside. She put the bottle on the kitchen bench and started sawing away. It was easier than she thought. Half the bottle broke off and the note fell out.

Feeling quite excited now, Nina unfolded and spread the piece of paper out on the counter, but there was no writing on it at all, just numbers. Ten numbers. She was puzzled now and feeling a bit let down. She had expected a message of some sort. She reread the numbers. looking for any other signs, but it was just a plain piece of paper, nothing else, no clue as to where it had come from.

Then she smiled. Of course. It was a mobile phone number. Nina reached for the phone. Without thinking, she started to dial, then quickly stopped. Was this the right thing to do? Perhaps she should take it to the police. Suppose it was important. Maybe someone was waiting for a call. She realised that none of this made any sense, the bottle could have just washed out to sea, and then what? Nothing would have happened if no one knew about it.

So Nina picked up the phone again and, before she could change her mind, dialled the number. It rang six times, she counted them, and then a recorded message with a robotic male voice said, 'Welcome to Astrology Unlimited. For your individual horoscope and a personal message, press 1 for Capricorn, 2 for Aquarius, 3 for Pisces,' and so it went until Sagittarius. There was a beep and silence, so Nina pressed 8 for Leo, and waited to hear what would happen next.

She was feeling the most excited she had been for a long time. What would the message be? She waited, scarcely able to breathe.

The voice came back and continued. 'Count your blessings and have a good day.'

Then the phone went dead. Nina continued holding it to her ear for a bit, but there was nothing else.

Frowning, she put the phone down. This is definitely weird, she thought, feeling a bit disappointed. She had wanted a cryptic message, or somebody telling her all about her future, at the very least a real person at the other end of the phone.

She wondered what the message was for the other months, and so tried ringing again, but there was no reply. Not even a ringing tone. Just silence on the other end.

Nina made herself a cup of tea and sat down to have a think. Then, having nothing better to do, she got a pen and pad and started to write down all her blessings. She felt a bit silly doing this, and at first couldn't think of anything to write, but once she got started she was surprised how long the list was, and by the time she couldn't think of any more, she was smiling. She felt happier than she had for a long time.

In fact, she was surprised to find she was having a really good day.

Monkey Business

Bobby John and Betty Jane were quite excited when they saw the 'Wanted' advertisement for a tame monkey to be used for a television commercial.

They looked at George, their pet. They had never been able to have children, and George had become a substitute son. They had raised him from a poor half-starved little scrap of a monkey who had been left an orphan after his mother had been killed, to a fine-looking nearly full-grown animal. He had a lovely cage in the backyard for when his humans went out, and a nice bed in the house where he spent most of his time watching TV.

George was quite happy with his lot. He was well fed. And he was spoiled by Betty Jane and Bobby John, who treated him like a child. He wore nappies for a long time but at last was getting used to using the toilet. He had never known any other life and didn't realise he was any different from other children. He responded to simple orders, was learning to use a spoon and was happy to be dressed up sometimes when he went for walks.

Bobby John and Betty Jane could do with some extra cash, so they made the phone call and got an appointment at the advertising studio. George was bathed and combed and dressed in his special shorts and shirt and off they went for the interview.

The advertisement was to be for a local business who wanted to demonstrate that they didn't indulge in monkey business. Which seemed simple enough. George just had to sit behind a desk throwing monopoly money up in the air.

George behaved well and sat still when ordered, exuberantly throwing money all over the desk.

The trouble started when another couple brought their monkey called Sally in for an interview at the same time. She looked adorable in her little pink tu tu. George stopped his antics and gazed mesmerised at Sally, who had escaped from her humans and decided to investigate by barging through the door to the room where George was being put through his paces.

Sally had previously lived in a sanctuary and so had seen other monkeys, so while seeing George stopped her in her tracks, she wasn't as surprised as George, who couldn't believe his eyes. His nose started twitching. He jumped up onto the desk, started leaping up and down and screeching, banging his chest, throwing papers and money all over the room, taking absolutely no notice of Bobby John, who was desperately trying to restrain him

Then Sally joined in, screeching and jumping up and down as well. Chairs became overturned in the efforts to restrain both monkeys. Absolute bedlam reigned and the advertising manager screamed at them all to get the hell out of his office.

Sally was too quick to be caught and raced out the door and down the long corridor with George following close behind. The doors on the lift at the end were starting to open and a couple getting out stared in startled surprise at the vision of two monkeys suddenly appearing in front of them. There were cries of horror as they quickly got out of the way.

Both monkeys hurried into the lift. George knew about lifts. The vets office was on the twelfth floor of a high-rise building, as were several friends of the family. Bobby John had taught him to press on a button and the doors would open or close, and the lift would move. So that is what he did.

By the time both sets of human minders breathlessly arrived at the lift, it was going up. They watched as it went right up to the top – to the twentieth floor. 'We'll catch them when they come down,' they said.

But the lift didn't come down. It stopped at the fifteenth floor and didn't move. Then it stopped at the tenth floor and went back up to the fifteenth.

Bobby John suggested they get the maintenance people to stop the lift and they would climb the stairs and catch them that way.

While they were debating what to do, the lift started moving again. They watched the floor numbers anxiously as it finally descended all the way and then stopped. Praying the monkeys would still be inside and not roaming around the building somewhere, they watched the doors open.

Two much calmer monkeys emerged, although Sally's tutu was in tatters, and George seemed to have a very smug look on his monkey face. Bobby John and Betty Jane were wondering what had just happened. This disruptive behaviour was quite out of character for George. And they wondered whether they should think about looking for a sanctuary with other monkeys, where the experts could care properly for him if he started getting too hard to handle.

But George settled down again, and things went back to normal, although the television job never happened, which was to be expected really.

A few weeks later, when it became apparent that Sally was pregnant, her humans were astonished. Of course they wondered who the father might be, but as Sally had spent time at the sanctuary sometimes for holidays they didn't worry too much about it. They were very happy at the thought of a new baby monkey to raise.

As for George, he didn't want any competition for his human's attention. He was quite happy and settled. He enjoyed being the centre of their universe. He made sure he didn't cause any problems and was his old docile contented self. He knew when he was on to a good thing.

But he did think about Sally sometimes.

Con Artist

Bert Jenkins was on the lookout for original art. He was a dealer who could, to quote himself, spot a fake at a hundred yards. He was on the lookout for bargains, and had customers who were relying on him to fill their orders, so when he saw Jimmy Chan's sign reading 'Genuine Original Oil Paintings For Sale' over the stall in the antique market, he decided to check it out.

Jimmy saw the tall man in the akubra approaching and readied himself for another sale to a gullible tourist.

Bert picked up one of the paintings. 'Good day,' he smiled at Jimmy, who nodded back and pointed to the picture.

'You like buy painting?' he asked.

Bert was peering closely at the picture, and studied it carefully for a moment, then tapped his finger on the signature at the bottom of the right-hand corner. It was nicely done, an oil painting of water lilies, in a rather decrepit frame.

'This is definitely not an original Monet,' he remarked. 'How much are you asking for it?'

'Yes, oliginal. Today, velly cheap, only two hunded dolla.'

Bert laughed in disbelief, and picked up another one. 'And a Turner?' He looked very closely at the larger painting, beautifully executed. An almost perfect copy. 'Where did you get these?' he asked Jimmy, who was finding it hard to maintain his inscrutable Chinese persona. This was the first time a customer had called him to account.

'I buy at auction,' he said now. 'All oliginal. Owner die,' he pronounced. 'You get bargain today.'

'I don't know what kind of a scam you're working,' Bert put the painting down, and picked up another one, 'but I can tell the difference between and original and a fake.' He stopped suddenly and studied the painting he had just picked up. Trying not to let Jimmy see the shiver of excitement that ran through his body like a small shock, he looked closely at the signature: Hans Heysen.

Jimmy Chan, feeling disgruntled, had moved away quickly to attend to another customer with an American accent who was proclaiming loudly to his wife what a wonderful bargain he had found. Jimmy was worried that the Australian was likely to put off any future sales to other customers.

Bert could hardly contain himself. He had actually found an original Hans Heysen. He looked closely at the signature. He was more familiar with Australian artists and was ninety-nine per cent sure that this was fair dinkum. You could always tell from the signature. The frame was quite ornate and nicely carved. He wondered whether Jimmy Chan knew he had a real original among all the other fakes. This would be worth far more than the $200 which was being asked for the others.

It didn't take long for his conscience to take a back seat. After all, he thought, business is business.

Bert waited until the American had left, proudly carrying his original painting, and then called Jimmy over. 'I like the frame on this one,' he said, 'so I'll make you an offer. They're quite expensive to buy new, but I can tidy this one up. The frame is worth more than the picture,' he added.

Jimmy Chan sighed. 'OK, you hard man, you try to cheat poor Chinese. How much you offer for flame?'

'I'll give you $50.' Bert knew this was pushing it a bit and wasn't surprised when Jimmy shook his head.

'No, not enough, no sale, this worth more.' He went to take the painting from Bert, who kept hold of it and stepped back.

'OK,' he gave a big sigh and gave in. 'I'll offer you $100 and that's final.' He hoped this would do it, and breathed a sigh of relief as the Chinese gentleman bowed his head in agreement.

He took the two fifty-dollar notes and stuffed them into the money pouch tied around his middle. He turned as another customer waited for his attention, and Bert tucked the painting under his arm and quickly left.

He made his way back home, where he couldn't wait to store his Heysen with the stack of others in the locked room in the cellar of his house. He had quite a few real originals in his collection, which was worth quite a considerable sum. He pulled out a small Heysen painting and put it on the table alongside his recent purchase. He found the magnifying glass and started a minute examination of both paintings. He had provenance for the first one. Unfortunately there was no way that old Chinese chap was going to produce one for this, he thought. He stopped his examination of the painting and trained the magnifying glass on the signature. He cursed, and threw the glass onto the table. The signature was forged. There was no doubt about it. Once he looked at the tiny details, he could see it. He had been well and truly conned. After a while, when he'd calmed down, Bert grinned to himself. That wily old bugger, he thought. But at least I got a half-decent frame.

Jimmy Chan packed up and went home, well pleased with the day's takings. He had made over a thousand dollars. He knocked on the door of his son Jack's room and entered.

Jack turned round, a paint brush in his hand and a half-finished painting on the easel in front of him. 'Hi, Dad,' he grinned. 'How'd you go today?'

Jimmy Chan removed the little cap he had been wearing and pulled off the fake pigtail. 'Pretty good, son.' He frowned a little. 'Had one chap today, though, who twigged. He spotted the fakes. I think it's time we moved on.' He patted Jack on his shoulder. 'How do you think you'd go with a couple of Pro Harts?'

'No worries, Dad.'

'Good,' said Jimmy, 'but in future, you'll have to be a bit more careful with the signatures.'

The Same Wavelength

Tommo and Ben were having a midlife crisis. They were lamenting the loss of their youth and were trying to think of something to do to regain their zest for living.

'I know,' said Tommo, 'let's go for a surf. Have you still got your surfboard?'

Ben looked a bit doubtful. 'Yeah, it's still stacked in the garage, I think. But gee, Tommo, it's been a long time. I don't know if I could still do it.'

Tommo whacked him on the back. 'Course you can. Mate, it's like riding a bike. You have to get back on. You never really forget how to do it.'

Ben still looked very doubtful. 'I dunno, mate. My legs aren't what they used to be.' Then he brightened up. 'Still, we'll never know if we don't give it a go, will we?'

'What about tomorrow morning then?' Tommo sounded excited. 'It's Saturday. The missus is taking the kids to see their grandmother. I'm supposed to be mowing the lawn. But the mower can always run out of petrol, can't it?' He winked at his mate, who understood exactly what he meant.

Next day, Tommo loaded his old surfboard on the back of the ute and called around to Ben's place. Ben had found his old board and had attempted to clean it up a bit and get rid of all the cobwebs that had collected over the years. He didn't have to worry about his wife. She had shot through a couple of years ago. Ben wasn't particularly fussed about that. There had been no kids to think about and he was currently enjoying getting back into the singles scene. Which was one reason he wanted to get fit and lose some of the flab he had noticed gathering around his middle lately.

Ben chucked his old surfboard onto the back of the ute, noticing a carton of beer stacked nicely into the corner. Good one, he thought.

The old mates reached a fairly deserted beach, parked, unloaded and made their way down on to the sand.

'Wind's getting up a bit,' Ben remarked. 'What about a beer while we see how it goes?'

'Good idea.' Tommo broke open a couple of beers.

They quietly sipped, contemplating the ocean. There were a couple of teenagers out there, getting regularly dumped into the water when they tried to get back onto their boards.

'Look at the height of that wave.' Ben sounded a bit doubtful. 'I dunno, mate. Looks a bit risky.'

He finished his beer and they sat on the sand, each trying to look more confident than they felt.

Tommo opened another beer. 'Well, what do think?' he said. 'Shall we give it a go?'

Ben didn't answer him for a long second. 'Let's just finish this beer and then we'll give it a try, OK?'

Tommo nodded, looking up at the sky. 'Looks like rain, though,' he remarked. 'Perhaps we'd better leave it for now until we get a good calm day. No need to rush things.'

Ben nodded quickly, before his mate could change his mind. He was quietly relieved, but didn't want to appear to be a wuss. 'What about dropping into the pub for a quick lunch then?' he said.

'Good idea, mate. We're on the same wavelength there, no worries.'

So they trudged back to the car park and carefully stowed their surfboards back into the ute.

Brief Encounter

There was an hour to wait before it was time to board her flight back to Sydney. Abigail glanced at her watch and decided to go for a coffee and pick up the latest *Readers Digest* to read on the plane.

She glanced at the elderly lady sitting opposite, who seemed to be falling asleep. She had slipped down in the chair, and the young couple sitting either side of her were carrying on a conversation between themselves, over the old lady's head. Then a seat became vacant beside the young woman and the young man moved across to her side.

Abigail couldn't help but hear some of the conversation. They appeared to having an argument and every now and again glanced at the elderly lady, who showed no signs of awareness.

'I can't do it any more,' the young woman was agitated. 'It's time someone else took on the responsibility.'

'Take it easy, Sal.' The young man touched her hand. 'We'll work something out.'

Abigail decided she didn't need to hear other people's problems. She picked up her carry-on bag, rose from her seat and made her way to the nearest kiosk. She bought a coffee and had a browse around the bookshop. The flight would soon be called, so she made her way back to her seat, which was still empty. People were beginning to get in line for the check-in. The old lady was still there, though. Alone. The young couple had disappeared. Abigail looked around; she couldn't see them anywhere. They definitely weren't in the queue. Maybe, she thought, they weren't with the old lady after all. Surely they wouldn't have just gone off and left her there.

Feeling a little perturbed, Abigail wavered. Should she do anything? Should she wake her up? She glanced around. No one was paying any attention. People were fussing with boarding passes, luggage, and listening to the announcements.

Suddenly deciding, she sat down beside the elderly lady and shook her gently on the arm. 'Excuse me,' she started, 'they're beginning to board the plane…'

She didn't have time to say any more. Surprisingly alert blue eyes opened and the lady gazed at Abigail.

'Yes, I know,' she said. Then she closed her eyes again and resettled herself in her seat.

Slightly nonplussed and feeling a bit embarrassed, Abigail hastily removed her hand and stood up. She made her way to the back of the queue. She was the last to board, but still couldn't resist saying something to the hostess checking her through. She pointed towards the seating area. 'That lady over there,' she told the hostess, 'is going to miss the flight.'

The hostess glanced over to where the woman was sitting, now all alone in the departure lounge. 'Oh yes,' she smiled, 'that's Emily Hobson. She often comes into the airport. Sometimes she brings her lunch.' She leaned forward, speaking quietly. 'She told me that she's writing a book and she often gets ideas for stories by listening to conversations. She pretends to be asleep so that people will leave her alone, and not assume that she's lost or abandoned.' The air hostess laughed. 'Between you and me, I think she comes because of the air conditioning. It's pretty hot out there today.'

As they watched, Emily Hobson took a package out of her shopping bag which had been stored under her seat, and began to unwrap a sandwich. She cast a glance over to the check-out desk, caught Abigail's eye, gave a big smile and a little wave. Abigail gave a little wave back.

'I'd better be going,' she said to the air hostess, then grabbed her boarding pass and hurried towards the tunnel leading to where her plane was waiting.

Don't Put All Your Eggs In One Basket…

Well, of course that would depend on how big your basket is, and how many eggs you've got. It also depends on where you bought them.

If you got them at the supermarket, they would probably be in a carton and not in a basket. If they are in a carton, it probably would be safer to carry them to your car in a shopping trolley. That is, if you have a car. If you have to go on the bus, then that could be a bit of a problem when you can't find a seat and have to stand. Unless you are luckily an elderly person, then someone might offer you a seat. This of course is not guaranteed either. Some people would probably get quite a thrill out of seeing someone drop their eggs, especially if they tipped out of the carton. Unless the eggs were dropped on or near them, like on their shoes or on their trousers. Then that could cause quite an uproar. It could lead to bus person rage and you could end up in an eggy mess.

If, however, you collected your eggs from somewhere that doesn't put them in cartons and you have to put them loose in a basket, then that gives you a whole new set of problems. You would need a big spacey basket so that the eggs don't knock into one another if you happened to trip or stumble whilst carrying them. It also would not be a good idea to take eggs in a basket on the bus. This would be quite disastrous and asking for trouble. Even if you managed to hold on to them safely, they would be visible to all and sundry. People would be eyeing your eggs with envy and you might feel compelled to offer them around until you have none left, although in this case of course, you wouldn't have to worry about dropping them.

So however you choose to transport your eggs, it can be quite an achievement to get them home without breaking any. To alleviate all these difficult and mostly unseen or anticipated problems, then it stands to reason that if you separate your eggs into two baskets or cartons then there is a fifty-fifty chance you will arrive with at least half of your eggs intact. Plus the weight is more evenly distributed. So don't put all your eggs in one basket. It makes you walk lopsided, which can cause muscle pain and maybe even give you arthritis in the future.

Of course, the best solution is to get chickens.

Chain Reaction

Fran's alarm clock had ceased to function and she hadn't got round to getting a new one. She relied on waking up in time, and sometimes did, but this morning she didn't. So when she left home in a rush to catch the bus, she was running late. Of course, the bus for once was running on time, and she watched it leave before she could reach the bus stop. That meant that she would be late for work.

Fran wondered whether to phone for a taxi, but it was the busiest time of the day and by the time it arrived, the next bus, due in half an hour, would be here. Besides which, she couldn't really afford a taxi. So she stressed and waited.

Fran worked in a boutique in the city and the owner Julie was waiting for Fran to arrive so that she could leave. She had had an agonising toothache all night and managed to get an early dentist appointment for nine luckily, due to a cancellation. Now she was getting crosser by the minute because Fran hadn't arrived at her usual time of eight-thirty. There were only the two of them, and Fran hadn't been there very long, so now Julie was wondering whether she was actually reliable. She couldn't just close the shop and leave because when Fran eventually arrived she wouldn't be able to open up. She had no key. This was due to the fact that Julie hadn't got around to having a spare one cut. The previous assistant had lost it. So she stressed and waited.

Meanwhile, the dentist Bob, who had a full list of patients that day, was looking anxiously at his watch. If his first patient was late, that would put him behind for the day, which meant irritable clients, and unless he could catch up, it would be another late night home, and his wife, who always had dinner ready for him, would be cranky. She was a fanatic for time keeping, which drove him crazy. So he stressed and waited, and eventually attended to the second patient, who had arrived early. She had a complicated procedure and took a long time, so that when Julie eventually arrived she had to wait quite a while.

By the time Julie got back to the shop, it was nearly lunchtime. She was in pain from the tooth extraction, and was in a nasty mood, especially when she found out that Fran hadn't make any sales all morning.

The dentist's wife Pat had had a busy day, shopping to make a special meal tonight. It was their wedding anniversary, though she was willing to bet that her husband had forgotten. But dinner was ready, table beautifully laid, wine and candles at the ready.

Unfortunately, Bob was now nearly an hour late getting home from work, and Pat waited and stressed, while dinner dried up and her suspicious thoughts went, not for the first time, to the blonde receptionist at the dentists surgery.

When Bob finally arrived home and saw the beautifully laid table and the expression on his wife's face, he suddenly remembered the anniversary, which he had forgotten again. He protested that he hadn't forgotten, it wasn't his fault he was late, and he hadn't had time to phone, but she was furious, and with great ceremony chucked the dinner in the bin, then went to the bedroom and locked the door.

Fran lasted another week before being sacked. She found another job closer to home and finally got another alarm clock.

Bob and Pat got divorced and Bob married his receptionist, who didn't cook but had other attributes which more than made up for it.

Forty Shades of Hay

The crop of lucerne was harvested. The bale-making machine had been put back into the shed and farmer Jack surveyed his paddock with a certain amount of pride. There they were, forty bales, rolled up neatly. Five rows of eight perfectly aligned drums of tightly packed beautiful fresh hay.

Jack was tired. It had been a big job. Tomorrow, he thought, he would see about stacking them up in the barn. He counted them again, just to recheck. He stood at the end of each row making sure they were all in line, which they were. It was important to Jack that everything was as it should be. There always had to be forty, no more, no less. If it turned out there was some surplus, he would strew it about the place. He would never make an extra drum. That would make it an uneven number and that would be too stressful; he would not be able to sleep. Today, however, and for now, Jack was happy, knowing that everything was in its rightful place and there was enough feed for his livestock to last a few months at least.

Inside the farmhouse, his wife Shirl was waiting for him to arrive home for his dinner. 'It's all finished then?' she called, without turning round from the stove as she heard him come in.

'Yep.' Jack didn't say much, just what was necessary.

'Yer dinner's ready,' she said, and as Jack washed his hands at the kitchen sink she placed his meal on the table, then she collected her own and switched on the little telly which was taking up part of the kitchen bench.

They both ate their meals in silence, watching the news and then the weather forecast. Heavy rain was forecast for their area tomorrow.

'I'll have to get them bales into the barn tomorrow.' Jack looked concerned. 'I don't want them setting saturated.'

His wife didn't say anything. She collected the plates and took them to the sink. She knew all about the bales. How big, how beautiful, how many. It was Jack's life. Growing the lucerne, worrying about the weather, the harvest, the livestock. There wasn't that much, mostly cows and a few horses. It was all her husband thought about, worked at, talked about. She knew that the bales had to be perfectly in line, and all the same size, or he would fret until he'd got them right. They had to go into the big barn in the same order, in particular rows. Sometimes she wondered if this was normal. All this worrying about bales of hay. Why, for instance, did they have to be in straight lines? It was all beyond her, so she got on with doing the dishes and Jack went back outside again to look up at the darkening sky, then collected his coat and went down to the paddock to count the bales again.

Next morning he was up early and down to the paddock before even having breakfast. It was starting to drizzle a bit and he pulled the hood of the parka up over his head. Suddenly, he came to a halt and looked closely at the lines of hay. Then he started to run down alongside the bales. When he came to the end, Jack stopped and stared. He blinked and rubbed his eyes in disbelief. The first row of bales had one missing at the end. There were seven instead of eight.

He looked around; maybe one had moved itself during the night, although how it would do that he didn't know. But there was no sight or sign of it.

'Some bastard,' he muttered. 'Some bastard's nicked it.'

He ran back home and managed to get inside before the rain came down properly. 'One's gone,' he shouted. 'Shirl? Where are you? I said one's gone.' He was quite distraught now, his voice getting higher with anxiety.

Shirl had heard him. She sighed. He sounded like he was going to have one of his turns and she went to fetch the bottle of pills. 'What's the matter?' she asked him.

'One's gone,' he said.

'What's gone?' She thought maybe one of the cows had disappeared.

'One of the bales is gone.' Jack had stopped shouting and was trembling with anger. 'I bet it's them bastard kids from up the road. They took one during the night. Where's my gun? I'll soon sort 'em out.'

Shirl laid a hand gently on his arm. 'Calm down, Jack,' she said, 'don't start getting worked up. ' She went to the sink and filled a glass with water. 'Here.' She handed it to him, with a tablet in the other hand. 'Take this, it'll make you feel better.'

Angrily, he slapped it out of her hand. 'No,' he shouted, 'no pills, not this time. I'm going to get the gun and sort them out for good.' He raged out of the room and a moment later shouted, 'OK, where is it, where's my gun? Where have you hidden it?'

Shirl recoiled as he stamped back, his hand raised. She started to dial a number on her mobile, and raised the phone high in the air as he tried to take it from her. 'He's having another one,' she managed to say to someone on the other end, before he managed to grab the phone and throw it across the room.

Then suddenly Jack slumped to the floor and curled up into the foetal position, distraught, twitching, and moaning, 'One's missing,' over and over, and he was still there ten minutes later when an ambulance arrived.

The ambos had been before, several times in fact, and one was a familiar face. 'Hi, Shirl,' he said brightly. 'What set him off this time?'

'A bale of hay's gone missing,' she said.

The ambo, Charlie, was checking Jack's pulse and vital signs. 'I think a sedative might be all he needs for now,' he said, 'just to calm him down, and then we'll get him into bed. He'd be better off here than going to the hospital again.' Charlie looked anxiously at Shirl, 'Can you manage him?'

She nodded.

'Just make sure he can't get his hands on the gun.

She nodded again. 'He won't find it.'

That dratted gun had been a worry for sure, she thought, but he had a farmer's licence and they needed it for foxes and ferals, and in case an animal had to be put down. She didn't think he would actually shoot someone, but when he got out of control, you never knew for sure. He had waved it around in the faces of the ambos one time when they had tried to get him into the ambulance that time when one of the cows went missing.

A couple of kilometres down the road, some young folks were preparing for a barn dance in a big woolshed. A bale of hay added to the atmosphere and ambience, and had been spray-painted with various colours. It looked quite splendid, serving as a seat where people could sit for photos.

It had been a good night.

'I hope he didn't miss it,' remarked one young fellow next morning, as they heaved the heavy bale back into Jack's paddock. 'After all, we only borrowed it for a day.'

They made sure it was straight in line with the others and in its proper place.

'Maybe we shouldn't have sprayed it,' said the other. 'It stands out a bit, doesn't it?'

They were young, and they laughed and went home.

Jack had slept on and off for most of the day and that evening heard the music in the distance. 'Someone's making a racket,' he grumbled.

To Shirl's relief, he seemed much calmer and, although he didn't mention the missing bale of hay, she knew he was grieving as if it was one of the cows had died. He didn't go down to the paddock that evening. It was as though he couldn't face looking at that empty space.

Next day was bright and sunny and after breakfast, with a resigned, but determined look, Jack strode out to do his usual chores and checks. He had only been gone a short while when Shirl's heart sank for moment as she heard him come running back.

'Shirl, Shirl!' but he was sounding happy and excited. 'Guess what?'

She looked at the happy smile on his normally worried, taciturn face. 'What?' she smiled back at him.

'It's back.' He was almost dancing with joy. 'It's back. The bale, it's back.' He stopped still, looking puzzled now. 'But it's got colours all over it. Someone's painted it.'

Shirl thought he was going ballistic again but he didn't. She realised that getting the bale back in its rightful place was more important than the paint.

And all he said was 'That's strange, isn't it?' Then he turned and went back out again.

Shirl closed her eyes for a moment and shook her head. Then went to get on with her morning chores.

Not So Hard of Hearing

Harold was going deaf. He hadn't actually accepted that fact yet. After all, he was only fifty years old. Not really old for these days, he told himself. In fact, he was, in his opinion, in the prime of his life. He was fit, he exercised sometimes, he wasn't much overweight, although he had to admit he had to watch his stomach these days. It bulged over his belt a bit more that it used to. He still had a fairly good head of hair and very little signs of grey. Unlike some of his contemporaries who were showing signs of baldness and fading colour. He only knew one person his age, an old mate, who was deaf, and he wore a hearing aid that was so obvious it was in his opinion, embarrassing, and of course there was his own father, who was after all, going on for ninety, so you would expect him to be deaf, and bald, which indeed he was.

Harold thought maybe he had ear wax but the doctor said his ears were pretty clean, and that he should go and get his hearing tested. But he resisted. In Harold's mind, hearing aids were only for old people. It's not too bad, he told himself. I can manage. It's only sometimes I have a bit of trouble understanding what people are talking about.

So he didn't go and get the test. Instead, he turned the TV up a bit and complained about how people mumbled these days. His wife Betty told him she thought he was going deaf, but he pretended not to hear. On this occasion, though, he had. His wife had a very loud voice and sometimes in the past he had wished he was deaf so that he couldn't hear her when she started raving on about something.

Now, though, it was becoming real and although, deep down, he knew he was being ridiculous, the thought of wearing a hearing aid filled him with dread. Harold was starting to get depressed. He stayed home more so that he didn't have to keep saying beg pardon or ask people to repeat themselves. He would just smile and nod as though he was interested in what they were saying.

It wasn't so bad at work. Harold was an accountant in a big insurance company. He had his own cubicle and used a computer for his work. He didn't have to use the phone very much, and if he heard it ring then he would go to the toilet, and when he wanted to relay a message to one of his workmates, he would send an email across the office like everyone else. If someone came to talk to him, he would pretend to be very busy, and he would smile and continue working until they got the hint and go away. At morning breaks, he would take a coffee to his desk, and at lunch would sit in the staff room and eat his sandwich whilst reading the newspaper or a book.

Harold started to lip-read a bit. He found that if he concentrated on people's mouths he could quite often make out what they were saying. Words like good morning or goodnight or thank you were easy. So he was getting by at work.

Home was a bit more difficult. When he came home from work, dinner was usually ready and the TV on. So they ate and watched TV and then afterwards, he would take the dog for a walk. If his wife went out to one of her club meetings (he noticed she seemed to be going out a lot lately), then he would watch TV with the subtitles on.

Harold noticed that Betty had stopped trying to talk to him; either that, he thought, or he just didn't hear her, which was strange because her loud voice had been one of the few sounds he could hear, even though most of the time he wasn't quite sure what she was talking about.

Then one day he came home from work and she was gone. She had left a note saying that she couldn't live with someone who she couldn't have a conversation with and that she was going to stay with her mother while she decided what to do. And that she had left his dinner in the oven.

Harold was flabbergasted. He never thought she would do that. He got the casserole out of the oven and switched the TV on. Then he realised the dog had gone. She must have taken Spot with her to her mother's. So he ate his dinner, making sure he left half for tomorrow, and then switched the TV off again. He had to think, to take stock of his life, and eventually, after taking everything into consideration, Harold made a momentous decision.

The next day he sent an email to the office advising them he was taking a sick day and made an appointment at the clinic where he knew they could give him a hearing test. He was lucky to get in, as there had been a cancellation that morning. After the examination, and much explanation from the doctor, who basically wrote everything down so that Harold could understand, and much waiting around, they produced a hearing aid for his right ear, which it seemed was a lot worse than the left one.

To Harold's amazement, it was quite small and fitted into his ear so well it was hardly noticeable. It was nothing like the large unsightly object that his old mate had worn. Then when they showed him how to use it, it was a revelation. He could hear everything so clearly, it was like being reborn. The doctor was beaming with delight at finally convincing Harold to have a hearing aid.

Well, that should have been the end of that really, except it wasn't. When it came down to it, Harold had got so used to the quiet that when he wore the hearing aid the noise was overwhelming.

When he returned to work next day, he decided to tell no one about it and he left it in his pocket. Everyone knew of course that Harold was hearing impaired, he had fooled no one with his various subterfuges, but no one had said anything. And because he rarely stopped to chat, they had given up trying to talk to him. Harold worked on as usual. He had come to enjoy the peace and quiet with no disturbances.

Occasionally he used the hearing aid. Like when he was called into the manager's office one day. This didn't happen very often unless it was for something serious. So he hoped there hadn't been anything wrong with his work. But Harold was pleasantly surprised. Apparently his work had been so outstanding that he was being offered a raise and a change to a larger cubicle with more responsibility. He didn't think the manager had even known his excellent accountant had a hearing problem.

Home was a different matter. Harold didn't relish the thought of having to cook his own dinner and do the laundry and so on, and over the past couple of weeks had dropped into the local pub occasionally for a meal on his way home from work. He had also discovered a laundromat not too far away. But he missed his wife sometimes. So Betty had a nice surprise when he called her one day and told her he had a hearing aid, and would she think about coming back home.

So she did. The trouble was that he wondered now whether having dinner cooked and the house cleaned was worth listening to the non-stop loud talking from Betty now that he could hear her.

So he started putting the earpiece in his pocket, and was managing fairly well, until one day when he was getting ready to go to work, he didn't respond to whatever it was she was talking about.

She peered closely at his ear and glared at him. 'You haven't got your hearing aid in, have you?' she shouted. 'You didn't hear a word I said, did you? What's the use of a hearing aid if you don't use it? I'm beginning to think you're not interested in anything I have to say.' And she stamped out of the room banging the door behind her.

Of course Harold didn't hear all of this, just the loud shouting. He picked up his briefcase and quietly left the house, got into his car, put his hearing aid in, found some music on the radio and went to work.

Beauty

She stood in her nightdress, bare footed, with black hair streaming behind her in the wind which had just sprung up. She must have been cold but was unaware of it when she had rushed outside. It was almost dark and she had been getting ready for an early night in bed with her book.

'Beauty,' she called, 'Beauty,' her voice high-pitched and sounding hysterical.

Then she saw a few people gathered on the pavement murmuring and pointing to something lying on the edge of the road.

'Oh no,' she cried, and pushed through the people, who parted and made way for her.

She dropped to her knees with a groan of anguish. 'Beauty, oh Beauty.' She looked up. 'What happened? did anyone see what happened?'

'She was chasing a cat,' a woman volunteered, 'and then the car came. It was going very fast. It braked for a moment but didn't stop. Just kept right on driving. You had left your gate open,' she added with a hint of disapproval.

'It looks like it's dead!' came another voice from behind.

The girl burst into tears. 'I didn't know she gate was open. I called and called her and she didn't come, then I heard the car screeching.' She cradled the dog's head in her arms then looked up and reached out to a man who was bent over beside her, peering closely at the dog. 'Is she really dead?' she asked him. 'Can you tell? I don't think she's breathing.'

The man put his hand over the dog's heart. Then he straightened up and smiled. 'I think she's only been knocked out, probably winded. I can't see any injury and there's no blood. Her heart is faint but she's still alive,' he added reassuringly. He felt all the legs with the expertise of someone who knew what he was doing, then he carefully picked the dog up. He looked at the girl, who was beginning to smile through her tears and who had suddenly realised that she was wearing next to nothing.

She rose to her feet and put one hand over her breasts, the other trying to hold her nightie down.

The small crowd was dispersing now as he said, 'Tell me which is your house and I'll carry her home for you.'

She pointed to a cottage a little way along the road. 'Just there,' she said, then she followed behind as he strode purposefully towards the open gate cradling the small dog in his arms. She was smiling now, and feeling totally embarrassed.

They went through the front door, which led directly into a small living room.

She indicated the chair with a doggie blanket on it. 'Just over there,' she said.

Beauty was beginning to stir now and her tail gave a forlorn little wag.

'She's going to be OK.' the man said. He was looking at the girl with interest, his eyes showing a glint of amusement. 'Perhaps you'd better get some clothes on, then I wouldn't say no to a cup of coffee.'

She stared at him for a moment, unable to say a word, then fled to another room, emerging five minutes later wearing jeans and a light jumper. She had got herself together now, and bent to fondle the dog's ears. 'Oh, Beauty,' she said, 'don't you ever give me a scare like that again.'

She went into the kitchen, where the man had found his way, and was opening cupboards, looking for cups. 'I don't even know your name,' she said, 'and, well, thank you so much for your help. Beauty means the world to me. I got her from the Animal Welfare League. No one wanted her because she was so ugly. That's why I called her Beauty so she wouldn't have an inferiority complex.' She stopped talking, aware that she was nervously babbling nonsense.

He put out his hand. 'Tom Banks, and you…?

'Jenny. Jenny Parker.'

They shook hands. 'How do you do,' they said together.

Tom turned back to the cupboard. 'Cups?' he asked.

He seemed to have made himself right at home, thought Jenny. She looked properly at him for the first time and saw a nondescript face with ordinary brown hair and a slightly crooked nose. Probably about her age. She liked what she saw, though, and by the way he was looking at her, it was pretty obvious he did too.

Beauty appeared, now seeming to be amazingly recovered. She looked from one to the other, gave a big tail wag followed by a short bark, then went to her bowl of water and took a long drink. Then turning round, she went to stand for a moment in front of Tom, who gave her head a ruffle, before returning to her bed in the other room.

'That's amazing,' remarked Jenny. 'I've never seen her take to a stranger so quickly.'

'She can probably smell other dogs,' he smiled. 'I'm a vet, I've just relocated from interstate. I live in the units around the corner, till I find somewhere more permanent. I was on my way to the servo up the road for the paper. He looked at his watch. I guess they're shut now.'

'Well, that's my fault. I'm sorry.' Jenny tried to look sorry, and failed.

'So where's the coffee?' he said.

The Olive Tree

The funeral was over. Grandpa Ben had been laid to rest and the family had the task of going through the house and sorting out all of his stuff. He had been a hoarder. Nothing had been thrown away, and most of the furniture was so old it was only fit for the second-hand dealer who was due to come the following day. The FOR SALE sign was already up in the front.

The hardest part was going through all the paperwork. Bills, receipts, brochures, every piece of paper had been kept. Even supermarket receipts. Grandpa had been a very private person. He believed in conspiracy theories and thought people were spying on him. There were even two security cameras outside.

My parents had tried in vain to persuade him to accept their help, to sort things out, to get his affairs in order, but he wouldn't have it.

He didn't even want them to visit. 'Leave me alone,' he'd say. 'I don't need help. I'll get around to it when I'm ready.'

So in the end they had left him to it.

Grandpa had lived alone for the past ten years, since Grandma had gone. I remember I heard Mum and Dad talking about her one day when they didn't know I was listening.

'Where's Grandma gone?' I had asked. 'Grandpa told us she's gone on a cruise,' said Mum, 'and you've got big ears,' and she said no more about it.

I thought it was a bit strange that Grandma would go on a cruise without telling Mum, but because it seemed Grandpa wasn't too bothered about it, then nobody else should be.

The thing was, you see, nobody thought about Grandma and Grandpa very much. We, my brother Jack and I, had school, Mum and Dad had work and there was always something going on. So Grandpa and Grandma were more or less left to get on with things without any interference from the rest of the family. Which in retrospect is a very sad thing to admit. But they lived over in the west, and we lived in the east, a long way away and it was quite expensive to fly over very often. To go by car could take up to a week, so there had been mainly just a phone call now and again to check they were doing OK. Grandpa had always been very independent. He said he was looking after himself. He always said he was fine and then didn't say much at all really. Even when the last time I talked to him on the phone all he said was 'How is school, and what grade are you in now?' and he sounded quite surprised when I told him I had left school last year.

Anyway, then he had this big heart attack and went to hospital. A doctor rang up and told Mum. He had fallen down in the garden and a neighbour had found him and called for an ambulance. Then he died before Mum could manage to go over to see him. So now we have the job of sorting everything out. I had flown over to WA with Mum and Dad for the funeral, and Jack had stayed with my Auntie Joan because he still had school.

So far, no one has found his will, if indeed he had ever made one.

'Not as though he had much to leave,' Mum remarked. 'There's just about enough for his funeral and not much else except the house, which will have to be demolished. It's full of white ants and in such a bad state of repair.'

We'd got some big cardboard boxes from the supermarket and were attempting to check out what to keep to go through later, and what to add to the bonfire we'd started, to get rid of all the rubbish. I was in charge of the bonfire, which was in a big old oil drum out the back. There was a bit of a wind and I had to stop things from flying about.

'Good job there's no fire ban on today,' Mum remarked, as she carried another box of rubbish outside, 'or we'd be in a right mess. There's so much stuff. I wonder why your Grandpa kept it all. None of it's any good.'

'P'raps he just liked to keep stuff to look at,' I said, 'to remind him of the old days, when Grandma lived here.' Then I asked something I had always wanted to know but never quite found the courage to ask. 'Mum, what happened to Grandma?'

She had started to feed stuff into the fire and said nothing for a moment, then she stopped and looked at me. 'I suppose you're old enough now to know about it. Well…' she paused and then went on, 'nobody knows. Everyone thought she'd gone on a cruise, but she never came back.'

Mum looked sad, and I was completely flabbergasted. How come nobody talked about this? I remembered well the last time I saw Grandma. I was seven years old and we had driven over to WA in the school holidays, It was her sixtieth birthday and I had persuaded Mum to buy a little olive tree for a present. Grandma had been so pleased and had planted it in the back garden.

'Where did she go then?' I asked now.

Mum looked thoughtful and tipped the rest of the boxful of rubbish into the fire. Then she turned to me. 'Grandpa told us she went on a cruise, but when he phoned and told us she hadn't come back, your dad and I went over to WA to try and find out what had happened. The police got involved and they had a big investigation but they couldn't find a trace of her. They concluded she had just left and probably changed her name. Most of her clothes and her passport had gone, and then they discovered she'd never even gone on a cruise to anywhere.'

I remembered now. My brother and I had stayed with Auntie Joan, my dad's sister, while my parents were away. We didn't really know what was going on. But we didn't worry too much either. We were just kids; the grown-ups never told us anything. We never asked about Grandma, because whenever the subject was brought up Mum got really upset. It was all a big mystery.

'But…' I started to say.

'No buts…' Mum patted my arm. 'It's been a long time. Ten years. I guess we'll never know. If she were alive, she'd have contacted me long ago. So we have to presume she's dead. So Sally, forget it, OK?'

I nodded. But it wasn't OK. How come they've never talked about this? I was feeling a bit angry. They should have told us. I wondered if my brother Jack had known. He was away on a school trip at the moment; lucky for him he had missed out on this big clean-up. I resolved to have a serious chat with him when he came back.

Then Dad was calling from inside the house. He sounded excited. 'I've found something.'

Mum and I hurried inside to see what all the fuss was about.

'I've found his diary,' Dad waved a small book in the air, 'at the back of the old bureau. It was filled up with all sorts of rubbish. Still no will, I'm afraid, but this might throw some light on a few things. Listen.' He started to read. '"8th May 2003: followed her today to see if she's telling lies about where she's going." Then 9th May. "That bloke from next door got his car out as soon as she went out and followed her down the road. Said she was going shopping. They've probably arranged to meet somewhere." Here's another one.' Dad was sounding a bit worried now. '"15th May: I suppose she thinks she's being so clever but she can't fool me. I know exactly what she's up to." And there's more of the same.'

He handed the book to Mum. 'Here, see for yourself.'

I peered over her shoulder to have a look. There was indeed more of the same. Hateful words about Grandma and accusing her of things which were unthinkable. Mum turned the pages. There were lots of gaps with nothing written, and then short notes about how he was keeping tabs. There was a month with nothing, and then some stuff about getting her just deserts.

The very last note had been on 1st December – about eight months from the start. He had written in large letters 'SHE'S GONE!' with a big asterisk after.

Mum had gone pale and had to sit down. 'That's about two weeks after she was supposed to go on a cruise.' Her voice faltered. 'Why would he write such awful stuff? Mum would never have done any of those things. She wasn't like that. I never thought there would have been anyone else. Not ever.' She looked up at Dad, who had his serious thinking face on. 'Do you think we should show this to the police?' she asked him.

She started to cry and I put my arm around her.

I looked at Dad. 'What do you reckon we should do, Dad?'

He always knew what was best and I had faith he would know what to do now.

He handed me the book. 'The bloke who used to live next door died five years ago, so we can't talk to him and nothing good can come from any of this. So Sally, what do you think? You're in charge of the bonfire.' He looked straight at me and I knew at once what I had to do.

I took the diary outside, had another quick look through in case we had missed something which might have been a clue, but there was nothing, so I chucked it in the fire. Then I watched it burn. I looked down the backyard where the olive tree was looking beautiful and flourishing nicely. The olives were almost ready to pick.

And I couldn't help wondering. What if?

Procrastination

Procrastination is the art of putting off something you don't particularly want to do but, knowing you have to do, using many excuses, or giving reasons, why you should be doing something else instead.

As was the case of Richard Dunby, who had promised his wife that he would fix the garden gate so that it would close properly, and she wouldn't have to tie a piece of string around it to keep it shut every time she went in or out. It had to stay shut to keep the dog in. Richard knew this. But they had not been married long and his wife Jill did not know yet that Richard was not much of a handyman.

Jill didn't want to be a nagging wife so she kept quiet for a few weeks, while Richard always had more pressing things to do than fix the gate.

The first time she mentioned it, Richard said he knew it had to be done but needed to go to the hardware shop to buy a new latch. And that he would definitely get around to it on the weekend. On Saturday, Richard had an upset tummy and spent quite a bit of time on the toilet, then Sunday recovering from whatever it was that ailed him. So Jill didn't mention the gate. After all, his health came first.

During that week when his wife brought up the subject, he gave her a cuddle. 'Next weekend love, I promise.'

So during the week, Jill continued to tie the string around the gate when she went out and tied it up again when she came back. Next weekend, she thought, finally he'll fix it. She trusted him to keep his word.

One evening that week, on his way home from work, he made a detour, called at the hardware store and after much haggling and asking advice from the salesman, bought a two-piece latch – half to go on the gatepost and the big bit to go on the gate. He put it on the bench in his shed alongside the never-been-used set of brand-new tools which someone had given him for Christmas years ago.

'I've picked up the gate latch,' he proudly told Jill that night. 'I'll fix it on the weekend.'

But next Saturday it was forty degrees. 'Much too hot to work outside,' remarked Richard and he stayed – 'doing work', he said – on his computer.

Next morning, he got up and went for a walk to the local shop. He took the dog, and when he came back he retied the string around the gate, left the dog in the yard and went inside to read the Sunday paper. Unfortunately, he had loosely tied a granny knot instead of a reef knot and it gradually undid itself. The dog, a pedigree poodle called Popsie, saw her chance for another walk, nudged the gate open, and disappeared up the road.

'Where's Popsie?' asked Jill.

'I left her in the yard,' replied Richard, busily rustling the paper. 'She didn't do her business yet.'

So it was an hour or so later that Jill went to call the dog in, and of course discovered the gate open and no Popsie.

After both of them had frantically run around the neighbourhood for nearly an hour, Popsie was found by a diligent neighbour who had recognised the dog and brought her back.

'Next time,' raged Jill, 'we may not be so lucky. If you had fixed that gate, this would never had happened.'

Richard had never heard his wife raise her voice before and was suitably chastened. His lovely quiet, compliant wife had turned into a veritable harpy. She thought the world of that dog, he knew, and so made excuses for her rage.

'I'm sorry,' he said. 'I'm really sorry. I'll go and fix it right away,' and quickly disappeared outside.

An hour later he came back in.

Jill looked up expectantly. 'Well, have you done it?'

'Well,' he said, 'I think need a drill. The nail won't go in. I think the wood's too hard.' He looked at his watch. 'Um…the shop's shut now, it's Sunday.'

Jill said nothing.

Next day, Richard came home rather late from work because he had called at the shop to pick up a drill, which was quite expensive.

He stopped at the gate in surprise. There was a brand-new latch, nicely fitted, which worked beautifully.

Jill looked happy and he thought a bit smug.

'So who fixed the latch then?' he asked in a slightly belligerent tone. After all, he had gone to all the trouble of buying a new drill.

'I phoned Hire a Handyman,' she said, 'and by the way, the latch you bought was the wrong size.' She plonked a sheet of paper in front of him. 'There's the bill for the new latch, and for Joe's time.'

'Who's Joe?'

'The handyman.'

Richard didn't much like the half-smile and the momentarily far away look in his wife's eyes just at that moment. He grunted, and went out to his shed, where he put the drill on the bench alongside the tools and the wrong-sized gate latch. He thought he should probably start using these tools for something. Like that bookshelf she was always on about.

Yes, he thought, maybe next weekend he'd start, or if something more important came up, then perhaps the following one. But he'd definitely do it. Definitely. But not right now. Right now it was time for dinner.

Secret Admirer

Jessica looked in amazement at the Valentine's card she had just found in the mailbox. This was the first time she had ever received such a thing. She could think of no one in her fairly restricted social life who would even contemplate sending her a Valentine's card.

She stood in bemusement at the garden gate looking at the beautiful heart decorated all around with roses. She had to admit it was a gorgeous card, and suddenly she felt embarrassed. She could feel a hot flush flooding up her neck and over her face. She looked around to see if anyone was watching, but the cul-de-sac where she lived was its usual quiet self. A few cars in driveways, no one out in the gardens and the only sound was that of the postie's motorbike disappearing in the distance.

She opened the card and read the rather unoriginal verse which said, 'Roses are red, violets are blue, but no one is quite as lovely as you,' and then looked closely at the message someone had written neatly underneath. 'From an admirer,' it said. 'From an admirer,' Jessica muttered to herself. Suddenly she felt angry. This was of course someone having a joke. It couldn't possibly be anything else. She almost tore it in half then and there, but instead put it back in the envelope and stuffed it into her pocket.

Back inside the house, Jessica put the card still in its envelope on the mantelpiece alongside the electricity bill propped up against the clock. She made a coffee and got stuck into the daily crossword she had been doing when she had heard the postie. Then she glanced at the mantelpiece. Something had occurred to her and she got up and looked at the envelope again. She had just realised there had been no postage stamp. She had assumed the postie had delivered it, but of course he couldn't have.

Jessica had a mental cold shiver. This was creepy. It must have been someone from around her neighbourhood. She put her crossword aside and settled down for a think. One by one, she mentally listed as many neighbours and acquaintances as she could think of and one by one eliminated them. There was just no one. Most of the neighbours had been there as long as she had – twenty to thirty years – and were retired. She didn't have much of a social life and the few friends she could think of certainly wouldn't go to the extreme of sending a Valentine's card, not even as a joke. Then she had a really strange thought. Was it even possible? Did she have a secret admirer?

Jessica's emotions were becoming decidedly mixed. They had gone from amused to angry, to mystified, and now strangely enough she was feeling just a little bit flattered. She looked at the clock. There was no time now for any more of these silly thoughts, she had to go down to the local shopping centre to pick up a few things She started to get ready, and then, unusually for her, stopped to have a long look at herself in the bathroom mirror.

Hair going grey, pulled back in a tight ponytail so she didn't have to worry about it, bushy eyebrows that hadn't been plucked for ages, dry skin, wrinkles. It was a face that hadn't had much care taken with it for a long time, and after much scrutiny she decided it made it all the more ludicrous that someone would send her a Valentine's card. Then for some inexplicable reason, she looked through the vanity drawer until she found an old pot of face cream and rubbed it all over her face. She found some tweezers and started with the eyebrows, but that was useless, it hurt too much, plus they didn't work properly, and she threw them back in the drawer. She took the elastic band off her hair and let it flow loose, but it had become just long and straggly, and untidy. She put the tie back on. Disgusting, she thought. Maybe she should get a haircut. It had been long time since she had visited a hairdresser. Then she found an old lipstick in the back of the drawer and carefully put it on. It looked strange, alien, unlike herself. Jessica sighed. If someone had thought her to be attractive enough to send a Valentine's card, then they must have needed glasses.

That day, instead of getting the groceries and going straight back home, Jessica stopped at the coffee shop and ordered a latte and one of the nice cakes she had always promised herself she would have one day. She watched all the people coming and going, recognising some.

Two of her neighbours came in and sat down at the next table, acknowledging her with a wave.

'Don't see you in here very often,' remarked Mary with a smile. 'Nice to see you out and about.'

Jessica returned the smile. 'Hello,' she said, realising that this was the first time she had actually spoken to anyone apart from sales people in the shopping complex.

She looked at Mary and her husband Bill. Friendly people, she thought, lovely neighbours, but definitely not the Valentine's card sending sort. She picked up her coffee and glanced at the magazine she had bought, so as not to encourage further conversation.

While sipping her coffee, Jesssica made a big decision. She decided to make an appointment at the hairdressers which just happened to be next door to the coffee shop. Luckily there had been a cancellation and she went in straight away, which was just as well, as she was about to change her mind if there had been a long wait. She gazed anxiously at the mirror as she watched her hair falling to the floor, but when finished, and the hairdresser fluffed her hair out around her face, Jessica couldn't quite believe her altered appearance. The modern cut framed and softened her face and was beautiful. She was overwhelmed and thanked the young hairdresser, who looked quite pleased with herself for bringing about such an amazing transformation.

Jessica felt confident enough now to go into the chemists, where she bought some eyebrow tweezers, some moisturising cream and a pale pink lipstick.

After that, she started stopping at the coffee shop more often, and when someone said good day to her she found herself having a chat instead of pretending to be busy doing something else, like writing notes on the pad she kept in her bag.

Yet in spite of scrutinising everyone and wondering, Jessica was no closer to discovering who had sent her the Valentine's card. It was a mystery indeed, but for some reason, she decided it didn't matter so much any more. She was feeling happier than she had in ages, more confident, and for the first time in years felt good about herself. Just knowing that someone else thought she was good enough to send a card to was enough. She hugged the secret to herself, and kept the card on the mantelpiece.

The Illiteracy Club

'I'm going to start a illiteracy club,' announced Chad to the small group of twelve and thirteen year old boys who met regularly in his dad's shed which had been turned into a games/music room.

It was Saturday afternoon, and much to his mum's amusement, Chad had put a sign outside the door which read 'NO ADULTS ALLOUED'.

'That sounds wrong,' said James. 'It should be *an* illiteracy club. You have to say *an* before a word starting with a vowel.'

Chad glared at him. 'Well, you would know, wouldn't you, smartie pants.' Chad only tolerated James because he was a good bass player. 'Anyway,' he continued, 'you probably wouldn't want to join. It's for people wot don't want to waste time on spelling, and reading and stuff, when there's much more intresting things to be doing.'

'Yeah,' interrupted Sam, another of the boys, who was setting up the drums in the corner, ready for the band practice. ''zactly.'

Chad nodded. 'Like music. If your goin' to be in a band and travel the world, you don't have time for all that useless stuff wot would interfere wiv the important things.'

'Well,' remarked James, 'who's going to be in your club then?'

'Well,' Chad was happy to explain, 'all them kids wot think reading and riting is a waste of time when they could be doing something that they like better, that they are good at. They should be ack...ack...'

'Acknowledged?' put in James helpfully.

Chad glanced at him suspiciously, 'Yes,' he said, 'acknowledged. They shouldn't be made to feel inferi...um, not good enough, just because they don't agree wiv all the rubbish teachers are making us learn in school. There should be a club where they can go where everybody is illiterate and can be proud of it instead of being ostr...um...ostra...'

'Ostracised?' put in James with a smirk.

Chad glared at him, then turned to the other boys. 'Who wants to be in the club then?' he asked them.

Sam, Bobby and the other boy Ken immediately raised their hands. 'Yeah,' they shouted.

'I know some other people who'd be good too,' Sam said.

'Yeah,' said Ken enthusiastically, 'and I know two girls who would.'

'No way.' Chad made a face of disgust. 'We don't want girls. This has to be a boys' club.'

'But girls are good at cooking and stuff,' Bobby interjected, 'and anyway, I saw Betty Jones chucking a book into a rubbish bin the other day when she thought no one was looking. I bet she's alliterate.'

'Orlright,' conceded Chad, 'girls can come but they have to prove they're illiterated.'

He went and sat down behind the drums. 'We'd better do some practice now and talk about the new club later.' He took a sheet of paper that James was handing out. 'What's this then?'

'It's a new song for us to learn,' James answered. 'Only three chords.'

'Great.' Chad peered closely at the sheet of music. 'What's it called then?' he asked him.

'The title's at the top,' said James with a little smirk. 'Can't you read it?'

There was a sudden hush from the others as they stopped fiddling with their instruments and waited for Chad's comeback.

'I don't need to know what it's called,' he said loftily, 'I just need to know the beat.' He started banging the drums and one by one they all joined in.'

Airport Encounters With Emily

Emily was sitting in the departure lounge at the airport. She often came here to sit and observe the behaviour of people when they were waiting for their flight. Sometimes they would ask her if she was all right and did she need any help. She always thanked them politely and told them she was fine. She had her notebook on her lap and wrote down snippets of conversation that she might overhear. It was research for the book she was currently writing, plus she enjoyed the atmosphere, not to mention the air conditioning. There were plenty of empty seats today. A plane had just left and the next lot of passengers were slowly arriving in dribs and drabs. Emily decided it was time for her morning coffee, so she put her writing pad back into her bag and made her way to the nearest coffee shop.

Henry Batts was going on the next flight to London and was feeling apprehensive. He didn't like flying. There had been the recent disaster of that aeroplane going down in the ocean which hadn't yet been located. He was suspicious of people wearing turbans and burkas and he glanced around, checking out the people around him. He made his way to the waiting area then stopped short, glancing at a black bag stowed under the seat he was about to sit on. At first he thought it must be something someone had forgotten, and then recoiled in horror as a terrible thought crossed his mind. Suppose it was a bomb!

He ventured forward again and bent to have a look. Just an innocent looking bag with a zip on the top and handle grips. He looked around. There was no one sitting nearby that he could ask whether perhaps they had noticed anyone sitting there. Henry wasn't one to get involved in anyone else's business and his next thought was to just go and sit somewhere else. But his conscience got the better of him. Suppose, just suppose it was a bomb, he could never forgive himself if he didn't tell someone. So he walked steadily over to the air hostesses chatting at the desk waiting for the next lot of passengers.

'Excuse me,' he started, 'there's a bag under the seat over there that perhaps someone's forgotten.'

The girls stopped their chat and turned to him.

'Where?' one of them asked.

'Over there.' Henry pointed.

She looked across, then walked towards the seat and peered underneath. She ran back to the desk looking slightly panicked and turning away from him, spoke quietly into her phone. She turned back to Henry. 'Thanks for letting us know,' she said.

Almost immediately two security guards were hurrying towards them. They stopped for a moment, looked under the seat and then one of them started shouting. 'Everybody out of this area, there's no need to panic, just gather your things and proceed quietly out to the main concourse.'

Everyone looked confused but did as they were told and started to get up and go back though the main door. The security guards were talking hurriedly into their phones and the two stewardesses followed quickly behind the passengers.

Of course there was much speculation. 'I wonder what's going on,' they said. 'Looks serious,' remarked another. 'I hope this doesn't affect the plane,' a man in a business suit said crossly. 'I'll miss my connection.' And so it went.

A child started screaming, probably because its mother was panicking. An elderly gentleman started shouting about the end being nigh.

Henry wondered what he had started and, much worried, went to the coffee shop where, as it happened, Emily was preparing to leave.

'Is this seat vacant?' Henry asked politely, indicating the seat opposite hers.

She smiled and nodded. Emily had finished her coffee and was trying to make out why passengers were streaming back out into the main airport area. 'What's going on?' she asked Henry. She didn't usually make conversation with complete strangers, she'd rather listen then talk, but this seemed to be a worthwhile reason to make such an observation.

'There's a security alert,' replied Henry, looking worried.

'Oh dear,' remarked Emily, getting out her notebook. 'What's happened then?'

'I don't know,' he replied. 'It seems they're waiting for the bomb squad. Hopefully it won't take too long, I don't want to miss my plane.' He looked at Emily. 'What flight are you booked on?'

'Oh,' she replied, 'I'm not going on a flight to anywhere, I'm just passing time.'

Henry gave her a curious glance but couldn't think of anything to say to that, so he said nothing.

Emily desperately wanted to go and see what was happening but decided it would be better to stay where she was.

Eventually the crowd, which had been pressed up against the window looking into the departure lounge, made way for two men wearing protective gear, presumably carrying equipment for detecting bombs. Everyone waited. There was an air of suppressed excitement, mixed with a little trepidation, plus general annoyance at this delay and upset to well organised travel plans.

'I hope you don't miss your plane,' said Emily politely, trying to make conversation. 'It's probably just a false alarm.' She regarded Henry's worried countenance, 'Don't worry. I'm sure they'll sort it all out in no time.'

'It's all my fault,' he burst out.

Emily was curious. 'What is?'

'I reported it.'

'Really? How sensible of you,' she said.

'Well, it might be nothing to worry about.' Henry was agitated. 'Just someone's bag that they had forgotten.'

Emily was beginning to have a bad feeling. 'What did you see exactly?' she asked now.

'Well,' he started. 'it was just a black bag, under a chair. So I told the hostess. I didn't expect all this carry on.' He waved a hand towards the crowd outside.

'Which chair?' Emily persisted.

He looked at her. 'Why? What does it matter which chair?' He was getting annoyed at this lady's questions.

'Just tell me.' Her voice had taken on an air of concern now, and Emily's suspicions were growing stronger. 'Which chair?' she repeated.

'Well,' Henry thought for a moment, 'it was the first chair on the second row back in the middle section.' He sat back, pleased with himself at remembering.

'Oh dear,' remarked Emily

'Why? What?' Henry bent forward over the table. 'Do you know something about it?' Hhe looked suspiciously at her. 'Do you know what's in that bag?'

''Yes,' she replied. 'It's mine. I left it there. I was only going for a coffee. I didn't expect to be very long.' Emily was looking more cross now than worried.

'Really?' Henry glanced outside where people were now making way for the bomb disposal unit who were very carefully carrying a big box, with presumably the bag inside, back out into the main part of the airport.

The loudspeakers were going now. 'Everyone may proceed back to the departure lounge.'

With a rush, people gathered up their belongings and made their way back,

'I told you,' a woman said. 'It was a false alarm.'

'Well, better be safe than sorry,' her friend replied.

Henry was standing up. He'd decided not to worry about coffee. He began organising his luggage. He turned to Emily. 'Well, what was in the bag then?'

'Just my stuff,' she said. 'Nothing dangerous. Just shopping and things.' She looked anxiously at the retreating security men. 'I suppose I should go and tell them.'

Henry laughed. 'Well, good luck with that,' and off he went to catch his plane, carefully avoiding looking under any seats.

Conscience

It was always worse at night. He tried to stay awake as long as possible, but eventually sleep would overtake conscious thought and the dreams would turn to nightmares. It was inside his head. He knew this, that they weren't real, but it didn't make any difference. He told himself that it was his subconscious repeating the horror over and over again. Logic told him that this was dreaming, but still he trembled and cried. He tried to wake himself up. He knew he was fighting a horror that was worse than anything he could have imagined. Worse, because it was all his own doing. It was his own fault. Sometimes he would wake, hands still trembling, his body covered in sweat, and he would lie still and silent, eyes darting from shadow to shadow in his bedroom, then he would watch the light between the window blinds, waiting for it to brighten with the coming the dawn.

In his heart, he knew there was only one way to make it stop. And until he did, the horror would keep repeating itself over and over again. It was her eyes that were the worst. He had seen the absolute terror in the eyes of the young girl as the headlights of his car beamed straight into her face, just as his car hit the bicycle. The scream that she gave penetrated the sound of his car's engine. It was dusk, very little traffic in the quiet suburb north of the city, and he had been driving home. She had come out of nowhere and he had been fiddling with the radio, trying to get some decent music. He had braked and backed up. Stepped out of the car, had a quick look around but saw no one. No other vehicles or pedestrians close by.

She was lying very still next to the bicycle, which had twisted handlebars and not much other damage that he could see, except for scraped paint. He bent over her for a second and he couldn't tell if she was alive or dead. He was aware of the bright purple helmet and blue jeans. A white sneaker had come off her foot and was some little distance away across the road.

And then he had panicked. He had had a few drinks at the pub and couldn't risk getting breath-tested, he knew he was over the limit, and not being able to drive would sound the death knell for his work, so instead of calling for an ambulance on his mobile phone, he'd got back into his car and drove away. He had stopped at one of the few telephone boxes still in the area and made an anonymous call reporting the accident.

He had watched the news. There had been no mention of a hit and run or of any fatality and he felt momentarily relieved, but now the nightmares had started and he knew himself for a coward. Night after night he relived that moment of impact and saw the terrified eyes and heard the open-mouthed scream.

It was two weeks before he started driving slowly through the neighbourhood and along that particular road every night after work. He thought he would recognise the girl if he saw her. He didn't know what he would say to her if he did. Maybe he just needed to check she was OK. Then maybe he could say sorry. He didn't know.

One day he left work early, pretending he had a doctor's appointment. The high school was close by and he had remembered seeing children waiting at the bus stop about three o'clock. He drove slowly past the school, where the speed limit was twenty-five, scanning the faces of the teenagers milling about, but they all looked the same in their uniforms. It was hopeless. He gave a little sigh and glanced ahead further along the road, and then his heart seemed to skip a beat. There was a red bicycle and a young person wearing a purple helmet. He passed the school zone then speeded up a bit until he was a little closer to her, then slowly followed.

He began muttering to himself, please let it be her. It must be. I'm sure it is. Then he braked, glad no one was close behind as he saw the girl abruptly turn left into the next street.

Keeping back now, he turned slowly, still following, and then watched as she stopped by a house, dismounted and lifted her bike over the kerb. She was about to open the gate when he drew up alongside.

He could hardly breathe, but before he could have second thoughts, he wound down the passenger side window and called out, 'Excuse me!'

She turned, looking at him with curiosity and a hint of caution. 'Yes?'

He got out of the car and walked round to the other side. He looked at her again and he knew it was the right girl. She looked fine, and he felt overcome with relief. Her eyes were steady now, not alarmed, as she regarded the portly middle-aged man with thinning hair and large glasses, behind which she could see eyes now welling with tears.

She leaned her bike up against the gate and stepped forward, concern now in her young face. 'Are you all right, sir? Can I help you?'

He faltered now as he struggled to find the words. 'I'm so sorry. It was me.'

She looked perplexed. 'I don't understand. Why are you sorry? Would you like me to get my dad?'

He tried again. Words coming out stronger now. 'No, no, that's not necessary. I just wanted to tell you, it was me. I hit you with my car. I'm so sorry,' he repeated, 'and I'm glad you're all right.' He glanced at the bike. 'And you had your bike fixed. It was my fault,' he added, 'and I should have waited to see if you were OK, but I didn't and I've been feeling bad ever since. I did call an ambulance, though.'

There, he thought, I've said it. He waited for the recriminations, the justified disgusting look of distain, and he bowed his head waiting for her to say something.

She said nothing for a moment, then, 'Oh, was that you?'

She sounded surprised. Not angry, as he had expected.

'How did you know it was me?' she asked then.

'I recognised your bike,' he replied, 'and your helmet.'

'Oh,' she smiled. Then half turned and nodded towards the house. 'Well, I never told them, and I never saw an ambulance.' she said now.

He blinked and stuttered a bit. 'Wh… What do you mean? You never told your parents?' he sounded perplexed. 'Why?'

'Because,' she lowered her voice, 'I wasn't supposed to be out so late. I'd stayed at the mall with my friends too long and my bike didn't have lights. Anyway,' she added, 'it was my fault. I was hurrying to get home and didn't look where I was going. If I'd told them I'd been hit by a car, then I'd have been in big trouble and they wouldn't have let me go out on my bike again, because according to them I'm irresponsible. In any case,' she indicated her leg, 'I was only scratched a bit, and my jeans were torn but they were old. It didn't matter. I had a big fright, though, and I think I screamed. I was scared and a bit winded for a bit. But I was OK. It's no big deal. In fact,' she smiled cheekily, 'it probably taught me a lesson, to be more careful in future.'

She stopped talking and regarded him gravely. 'My dad thinks I got a puncture and fell off my bike, so you aren't going to say anything are you?' She looked a little anxious. 'I'm sorry you were worried, though, and thank you for telling me.'

She was being so polite and kind, he found himself wanting to give her a big hug, but he stepped back a pace and shook his head. 'No,' he managed a smile. 'They won't hear anything from me.'

The front door opened then, and a man's voice called out. 'Jess, it's time you were home. Who's that you're talking to?'

'No one, Dad,' she called back, 'just someone asking directions.' She quickly opened the garden gate and wheeled her bike through and up the path. She looked back for a moment, gave a brief smile, then disappeared into the house.

He got back into his car and started the engine. He wiped his face, then put on his seat belt. The relief he felt was so overwhelming, he had to sit for a moment, before getting himself together and moving off.

'Thank you,' he said to Jess, who couldn't hear him, and to the universe in general. An enormous feeling of peace invaded his being.

He put the car into gear and headed home.

Gazza

I was sitting up the front of the train and had two seats to myself, which was lucky as the carriage was filling up fast. Two young people were seated across the aisle with iPads on their laps and earphones dangling. They were travelling together, but separated by technology. No conversation. How strange, I thought, nobody talks to anyone any more.

I was on my way home. It was evening and almost dark outside. I was pleased to see the railway security guards patrolling up and down the carriage, keeping an eye out for yahoos and general trouble-makers, but it was strangely quiet apart from the rattle of the train.

Then you sat down beside me and I had to move over as you were so big. I gave a sideways glance and saw the tatts and the earring, the unkempt straggly hair. You were scary-looking and I edged as far away as I could until I was squashed up against the window.

I got out my *Readers Digest*, which I always carried when travelling. It didn't take up much room in my bag. I thought maybe I should get one of those iPad things and be like everyone else, then just as quickly dismissed the thought. I felt comfortable with my book. It didn't need recharging for a start.

So it was just another boring train trip until suddenly, unexpectedly, there was this great piercing screech of metal grating upon metal. The train abruptly began to slow down, and then the carriage started tipping sideways. People were beginning to panic, shouting in fear and trying to hold on to their seats. Then I saw the carriage that had been in the front of ours suddenly appear through the opposite window. I remember being flung from my seat and pain and then nothing else.

I don't know how long I lay there, but when I woke up and gradually came to my senses I found myself lying next to a broken window. I was covered in glass fragments. My head hurt and I struggled to remember what had happened. I tried to move my arms and legs. My arms were free but I realised I couldn't move my legs. Panic engulfed my being and I looked to see if there was anyone else nearby, but there was nobody, just a pile of twisted steel and broken seats. I was feeling alone and in pain and so scared. I looked for my bag with the phone inside, but it had gone.

Then suddenly I heard a voice, but couldn't see where it was coming from. 'Is anybody there?' someone was calling.

For a moment I couldn't speak. I put a hand to my head and it came away red and sticky. I was bleeding. I tried to move my legs again but they were jammed under something. I realised I was lying on the side of the carriage where the young couple had been sitting. I wondered if they had gone out of the window. I hoped they were OK.

I found my voice. 'Yes, I'm here.' It came out small and weak. 'But my legs are stuck. I can't move.'

'OK,' said the voice of a man; it sounded strong and confident. 'I'll see if I can find you. Keep talking.'

I was under the seat I had been sitting on. The other side of the carriage was now on the top.

'Where are you?' I called, and then I saw something move. An arm appeared from the wreckage alongside me, so I reached out and grabbed your hand. I saw the tatts on the back. LOVE it spelt out on each knuckle. Then I knew who you were. And I was never so pleased to see anyone in all my life.

'I'm here,' I said almost sobbing with relief.

Then you pushed the bits of steel and chairs and stuff aside and gradually made your way through until you were half sitting and half lying beside me. And then you smiled. And I thought it was the most beautiful smile I had ever seen.

'Don't worry,' you said, 'I'm sure they'll have us out of here in no time.' You looked at the broken seat lying on top of my legs, then you took a deep breath and gave an almighty shove and lifted it up, just a little bit but enough to pull my legs out. My pants were torn and there was a fair bit of blood, but nothing seemed to be broken.

'Thanks,' I managed to say, realising at the same time that one of your legs looked funny and twisted. 'Your leg,' I pointed. 'I think it's broken.'

'Yes, it probably is,' you grimaced. You must have been in such pain but you pretended you weren't.

So then we waited, listening for sounds of rescue. We could hear other people crying and yelling for help, but could see no one. There was the occasional shift of something moving and the fear of more wreckage falling down on top of us. You found your phone still in your pocket and calmly called some numbers and then you kept talking to me. You told me your name was Gazza and I told you my name was Jane, I told you about my family and you told me about your band and the gig you wouldn't now be playing at tonight.

Every time I felt like dropping off to sleep you shook me awake. 'Stay awake,' you said. 'You must stay awake, you may have concussion.'

So I would rouse myself and think of something else to talk about. It seemed for ever before we heard the ambulance's sirens but it probably wasn't that long. Then we waited for heavy machinery to come with cranes and then the jaws of life were wrenching at the twisted metal, until at last we could breathe the night air. Then gentle hands were lifting us out, and before I could thank you or say goodbye you had gone.

I haven't seen you since, and I hope this letter finds you. I wanted to thank you for your kindness, your caring and help which kept me alive. I don't think I would have made it if you hadn't been there.

So thank you, Gazza.